ALEXANDRIA CUNNINGHAM

Hot Tea and Laughter

First published by Funky Fresh Nerds 2021

Copyright © 2021 by Alexandria Cunningham

All rights reserved. No part of this publication may be reproduced, stored or transmitted in any form or by any means, electronic, mechanical, photocopying, recording, scanning, or otherwise without written permission from the publisher. It is illegal to copy this book, post it to a website, or distribute it by any other means without permission.

This novel is entirely a work of fiction. The names, characters and incidents portrayed in it are the work of the author's imagination. Any resemblance to actual persons, living or dead, events or localities is entirely coincidental.

Designations used by companies to distinguish their products are often claimed as trademarks. All brand names and product names used in this book and on its cover are trade names, service marks, trademarks and registered trademarks of their respective owners. The publishers and the book are not associated with any product or vendor mentioned in this book. None of the companies referenced within the book have endorsed the book.

Library of Congress Control Number: 2020921530

First edition

ISBN: 978-0-578-77769-6

Editing by Shelley Mascia

This book was professionally typeset on Reedsy. Find out more at reedsy.com

To my husband, Kirstan, may you continue to be my "hot tea and laughter" as we continue along this journey called life. To those in the hallway waiting for the next door to open, keep walking. Your calling could be right around the corner.

Contents

Acknowledgement	ii
Brew	1
Tea Time	8
Sugar Cane	16
Mint	23
Bliss	30
Sage	33
Butterscotch	40
Gingerly	48
Sommelier	51
Aroma	57
Foreign	62
Meh	69
Milk	73
Wither	76
Refresh	80
Reliant	89
About the Author	92
Also by Alexandria Cunningham	93

Acknowledgement

God, thank you for "Hot Tea and Laughter!" You have been so incredible through this writing journey, and for that, I am grateful. When I wanted to give up, you showed me what it meant to confess the word and believe. Faith produced this book. Thank you for blessing the work of my hands.

Shelley, thank you for being an amazing editor and friend. You are so encouraging and great at what you do.

Tierra, you are a gem, and I cherish our friendship. Thank you for teaching me that no matter how nice a person you may believe you are, you were a villain in someone's life. May we live out our lives to be heroes instead.

Daniel, my "big brother," thank you for your laughs and love. You and Tierra were there in the beginning when "Hot Tea and Laughter" was merely a chapter title in a stack of my unwritten books.

Kiera, you are the friend that I prayed to God for. I have enjoyed having you alongside me throughout this writing journey. Thank you for your prayers and constant words of encouragement.

Natasha, my inspiring teammate, sister-friend, and listening ear. Thank you for allowing me to constantly read passages from the book and share cover designs throughout the night until it was just right.

Tia Dubose, thank you for being my hairstylist, counselor, and sister-friend. I always leave your chair better than I came.

TJ Smith, thank you for guiding me toward the next steps of my educational journey when I felt complacent and wanted something more.

Steak. Shake. Bye, Bae.

Brew

*J*ust *dive in headfirst, simmer down Prue,* I thought as butterflies churn my stomach. He was standing there on the sidewalk as if the very essence of my existence were but a mist floating in the air. He did not even notice me, yet I didn't care. I sat back in my chair, chin resting on my fist as I inhaled deeply, hoping to swallow the frog in my throat. *Why doesn't he notice me?* I sighed and continue to stare. I dared not look away; he does not even know I am here.

"Hey, girl, let me guess, Cupid has struck you with his arrow again," Connor snorted, snapping her fingers in front of my eyes, bringing me crashing back to Earth. "He must be being paid overtime because this is the third time this week that you are absolutely speechless."

"You say something?" I asked.

"Nope, not at all," Connor shook her head.

I shook the cobwebs from my head and placed several teapots of shapes, sizes, and colors in front of her at the table. "What would you like to try today? I have been working on something new," I motioned to a yellow teapot that had Roman's Tea Bliss, Manhattan, NY, stamped on the bottom of it. "Try this one."

Connor took a sip and looked up at me with sparkling eyes.

"Oh, this is pretty good. What do you call it?"

I giggled. "I think I'll call it blackberry psalmist because every time I see that blackberry lemon drop, my heart skips a beat."

Connor laughed again. "Girl, you bugging'. But I can't front, he does look good, and this tea is delicious. What's in it? It's a blackberry blend with a hint of lemon, honey, and vanilla.' She took another, longer sip. "You outdid yourself with this one! This may be one of my new top five."

"Thanks, girl, I like it too. Did you see the new teapot my great aunt sent from Cali?" I held up a shiny black lacquered china teapot for her to see.

"Oh wow, that's beautiful," she said, admiring the way the light hit it.

I smiled and held it in my hand for another minute, admiring it. "Yeah, I think I'll keep it on the shelf for a while."

"Cool," Connor paused for a second, then grinned widely. "Girl, let me tell you about what happened to me today. Chris dropped by while I was in the middle of a conference meeting."

I pulled a frown, thinking. "Chris? Like Chris that took you on a date and never called back?"

She leaned back in her chair. "Girl, yes. Takin bout he had a lot going on but wanted to ask me out tonight for a date."

"So, what did you say?" I asked, putting away the rest of the teapots behind the counter, on the warmer bar. "Are you going?"

"Child, I don't know. I guess you know I love to eat. And if I don't have to cook tonight, then why not."

"Alright." I laughed, wiping down some of the counters. "Don't hurt him now, girl."

"Why you say that?"

I snorted. "Because I know his pockets are deep, and you really like to eat."

"Shut up. You're wrong for that."

"Well, it's the truth," I waved to her as she got up and left out of the door. "Love you, girl," I called as the door closed behind her.

As I watched her walk away, I thought about how Connor Daniels is cool. She's been down since forever. Some friends are seasonal, but Connor, she's my ride or die. Sometimes I get caught up with my own infatuations that I forget to cross-examine the tea house. This place is like my second home, and my customers are like my guests. I always want them to feel wanted and as if they belong.

Take Mrs. Judy, for instance. She's been coming here so long that she is a staple at the tea house. Judy Simpson is a retired judge from West Virginia, twice widowed, and has a knack for good tea and eloquently reading your rights if you cross her. I like Mrs. Judy. She's just the right amount of sass and class. She's like the cool Aunt that you long to see during the holidays. You should always keep a good older mentor around.

All seems well in the tea house today. Soft jazz plays over the speakers as the cars and pedestrians move quickly outside the shop. The sweet aroma of mint fills the air as I muster up a fresh cup of peppermint tea for Mr. Tom.

He's a quiet man, always reading mysteries and thrillers. I wonder what his life was like in his younger days. Everyone has a story to tell. One of the reasons I enjoy making tea for people is that I can automatically read their personality, learn about the day they've had, or set the tone for their day.

You know the saying, eyes are windows to the soul, well I also believe that about the tea people drink. As long as you're still breathing, there's a tea to drink and a life story to tell. I'm only eighteen years old. My story is just getting good. See, unlike my friends, I was the only one in my class to take a gap year after graduation to figure out what I wanted to do, have fun, and just be me. I've never felt so free.

I have always been inspired by the scent of fresh tea and what could be. No one gets to decide my fate but me. Well, I say that, but the gap year really chose me. I wasn't aware of my choices…I didn't take college road trips, wasn't offered major scholarships, or even a college or university legacy. You may look at this as a negative and ask *girl, how are you so calm?* Trust me. I did not always feel this way.

When time is ticking, and you don't have a plan, what do you do? Instead of spiraling out of control and try to figure out where you're going, I decided to figure it out as I go. My friend, Connor, on the other hand, detailed everything she wanted to do in life. I don't operate like that, and I learned a long time ago that it's perfectly okay.

I refuse to become a victim of my circumstances, which has placed me in hot water. Instead, I choose to turn that hot water into tea. I consider myself to be a bit of a "tea barista." I'm not quite a "tea master."

Roman's Tea Bliss is a beautiful tea house in the middle of the city. There's actually a yoga studio upstairs above the house, hence the name. Roman, the owner, is the ultimate tea master and a trained yogi that leads sessions throughout the week. I often skip lunch so that I can join him and relax. Mom and I take yoga together on our self-care Wednesdays. She always says that hump days are the best days for mountain poses and three scoops of ice cream from our local creamery afterward.

My mom is a bit eccentric, which is always surprising when people find out that she was born and raised right in the heart of Detroit, Michigan. Mom is definitely a "snack," although she likes to say that she's the whole meal. She's 5"7," skin like a smooth copper penny and skinny as can be with thick black curly hair. I get my features from my dad, I guess. He took off after my mom found out she was pregnant. Once my dad took off, my mom packed the two of us up and moved us to Brooklyn, New York.

I wouldn't know who my dad was if he came into the teahouse and stared me right in the face. Mom has never shown me not even one picture of him. I guess it was her way of protecting me. It wouldn't surprise me. She's so good like that. Always looking out for others, especially me. I hope to be half the woman my mom is.

I can't help but wonder what it would have been like to have grown up with two parents in the household, though, if my dad and I have the same laugh. Or if both of our eyes squint alike, tightly when we laugh. I guess that's why I used to hang out at Connor's house so much. I love the idea that she was raised in a house with both parents and—a brother. She and her family would always eat together at the table. Mom and I usually eat on our giant floor pillows, with our legs crossed Indian style. Connor's family also had a family game night every Friday night. She would always invite Mila and me to join. It was so much fun.

I'm 4"11" and shaped like a pear. My shoulder-length hair is brown, thick, and curly, not like my mom's, whose hair reaches her tail bone. I love my skin. It's the shade of honey. My mom always says that I'm her honey drop that's been bronzed by the sun because I have freckles across my face.

I just moved to Manhattan to be closer to the tea house a few weeks ago. So far, so good. I live in a studio apartment filled with so many plants that you would think that I was housing my own greenhouse. I also have the sweetest gray cat named Jasmine to keep me company. I love people watching; I often ask myself, are they happy, what do they do for a living, where have they traveled, and what mistakes have they made along the way. I like to take chances, yet I play it safe by learning what not to do.

Connor, on the other hand, with all her planning, always plans out her risks. For our senior trip, she was the only one that went skydiving. I don't know about you, but I like to keep my feet planted on the ground. Connor is going off to college in about a week. She'll be attending Clark-Atlanta in Atlanta, Georgia, just like her parents. Mr. Daniels majored in Criminal Justice, while Mrs. Daniels majored in Business Administration. The two met on the quad while having lunch with their friends. The rest is history. Mr. and Mrs. Daniels are basically living the "American Dream" in a three-story home. Conner, and her brother Drew, were major athletes in almost every sport and never gotten so much of a hangnail without their parents knowing.

Drew and Conner are eleven months apart, but you would swear that they were twins. They consider themselves best friends for sure. I used to find myself idolizing their relationship. I guess it's the longing for having someone there that understands me and always has my back. Being the only child can get lonely. I'm constantly wondering what my life would be like if I, too, had a sibling. Having close friends are dope though, Connor and Mila are like my sisters. I am so thankful for them.

Mila has always been the easy-going type. She can turn any rainy day into a ray of sunshine. I was so shocked when she announced she would be going off to the Airforce. I never saw her as a military type. Mila seems so cool and collected about her decision. Deep down, I feel as though she's afraid. I wonder if she'll be treated right, can handle the pressure of being yelled at by the Airmen and other officers, and if she'll miss home. Whenever she gets back, I'll have the perfect tea for her. Something soothing and calm, to give her peace of the path she's chosen and the joy of being home.

The house is closing soon. I didn't even get a chance to ask the blackberry lemon drop if he wanted a refill, let alone his name. All is calm in the house again. Guests no longer come through the door, the shoes along the sidewalk have come to a halt, and the melodies that filled this room has drifted away. Until tomorrow, the tea begins anew.

Tea Time

Ugh. I absolutely hate waking up to Jasmine's bushy furry tail up my nose. It isn't enough that the rays of the sun are beaming through the blinds. Jasmine has to make sure she wakes me up as well. It's Saturday, which means a free day for me and "tea time" with my girls. I'm a bit of a morning person. I love the opportunity of a brand-new day. The sweet sounds of Nora Jones fill my apartment as I brew a pot of water for some breakfast tea to go along with my avocado toast.

These last two weeks of summer is sure to be filled with adventure. I don't know what I'm going to do without my girls around. I'm looking forward to lunch today. I'm always down for some good food from a new place. Connor is finishing up her summer internship with a few higher-ups at a marketing firm upstate. She and Mila will be taking the train to meet me later.

I better get a move on if I'm going to make lunch on time. I always take forever to get dressed, then wind up wearing the same ole thing, burnt orange Jeanie pants with a white crop top and rope sandals. I know what you're thinking, and yes, I'm a lot like my mom. What can I say? I'm a free spirit.

As I walk along the sidewalk to the restaurant, I enjoy being captivated by the sun. I love how the sun beams onto my face and warms my thick curly hair. I love walking; I get to people watch and imagine where they're going, knowing that the possibilities are endless for them and me, well in my mind anyway.

"Hi, Mr. Peterson!" I said, greeting one of my regular customers as he sweeps the sidewalk in front of his bakery.

"Hey gal, how are you today."

"I'm fine getting out into the city for a bit."

"Well, enjoy. There are lots you still haven't seen, I'm sure."

"Will do."

Mr. Peterson owns the bakery over on 47th street west. He's the cutest little Italian man I've ever seen. He's one of the first people I met when I came to Manhattan. My mom knew him for years. He promised her he would look out for me while I'm here. My mom knows many people. She owns a pottery shop back in Brooklyn. Most people know her from art shows and galas.

Man, my calves are burning, but I've finally reached the restaurant called the Mediterranean by the Sea. I'm excited because this will be the first time any of us have tried Mediterranean food. It's such a cool little shop, painted light blue like the sea with ocean sounds as the background music. I love the way it's set up. I grab one of the high tables along the front window of the restaurant. Mom always taught me to sit where I can see the door, and what better view I will have than this huge picture window.

"Hey, Hey!" Connor's distinct voice greeted me.

"What's up, chicks!"

I hugged them quickly and grabbed Connor by the arm. "Get over here and pour this tea, miss Connor. You know I've been waiting to hear about this date. Mila, I'm sure you've already heard it on your ride over."

Connor laughed. "Don't do us like that, Prue. We actually waited so that we could all hear it together."

"Please, don't even act like you're thinking about me. I'm sure Connor didn't want to tell it twice," I said as they joined me at the table.

Connor put her hand over her chest. "Ow, my Sista, that hurts, but you know me so well."

"Well, anyway, get on with it," Mila said.

"Okay, so I must say the date went a lot different from what I thought it was going to be. Chris was the perfect gentleman. He took us to a restaurant up on Durer. It was so classy. He had made reservations and everything. I was quite impressed. He ordered for us both. It was some exotic food I have never heard of before. He ordered a bottle of wine with him being twenty-one and all, don't worry, I had sparkling water. Girl, it was all that. Brother was fine, looking all Kofi Siriboe like and smelling so good. Your girl was beyond captivated by his smooth-talking, sweet-smelling self. I couldn't stop grinning, and you know I don't like showing that many teeth."

"Connor, you have absolutely been smitten," Mila said as Connor took a long drink of ice water.

"I know, right, but are you going to continue to interrupt, or do you want to hear about the rest of the night?"

"Sorry, continue, girl."

"Well, after we left the restaurant, we went walking around

the park before he took me home. It was the perfect night. When we reached the steps to say goodnight, I was ready to move in and kiss brother man. Right when we were both moving closer to one another, palms sweating from holding hands gently but so tight, Daddy opened the door and said in the deepest voice like the Daddy from Lion King, "Tell this gentleman goodnight, Connor."

"OH, No! How embarrassing," Mila squealed.

"I would have just fainted."

"I know, right. I told Chris goodnight and ran up to my room as fast as I could. You know Daddy would have drilled me all night about the date. Luckily, my mom handed him a cup of coffee and made him back off."

I sighed and placed my hands under my chin, "Girl, it sounds like you had a wonderful time despite "Big Daddy" coming to ruin your good night kiss.

"It was the best. I definitely plan to see him again before I leave for school."

"So, what's up, what's good with y'all?" Connor said, picking up the menu.

"Well, you know me, working out and running hills to get ready for basic training," Mila flexed her shoulders.

"Mila, dang girl. They got you training before basic training. That's crazy." I picked up my menu too.

"Well, it's better that I get it in now before they start screaming in my face for not finishing a pushup."

"Yeah, you right. Good for you, girl."

"What about you Prue, what's new?"

I sighed and shrugged. "Well, you know, the same ole, same ole. Adventuring around the city and coming up with new things to add to the menu. My mom should be coming by soon to add a few more things to my apartment. Baby wants to add an alarm system with cameras and everything."

"Oh wow, at least you'll feel safe," Connor whistled.

" Yeah, for sure," Mila added.

"Anyways, can we order? I'm starving," Connor said.

"Girl, you are always starving, but today I'm with you. My workouts and eating plan has me feeling famished."

"This looks good," I said, pointing to a tasty looking pasta dish.

"I'm glad this menu has pictures because you know I don't like to eat anything that looks too weird," Connor sniffed.

"Girl, you always tripping. Branch out a little bit. You may like it," I said.

"Prue, everybody ain't you. You'll eat anything."

"I can't argue with you there. You know I'll try almost anything once."

"Hi ladies, are you ready to order?" A young waiter with eyes the color of the walls came up to us.

"Yes, I'll have the number one with water."

"I'll have the number seven with an apple juice."

"And I'll have your number sixteen with another water and extra sauce."

"Alright, I'll get your drinks right over once I put your order in."

As the waiter moved away from our table, my heart sank into my stomach. There he was, the guy from the teahouse, standing outside on the sidewalk talking to some people. I froze, unable to even blink. I wonder where he's going or if he lives nearby. I sure hope he comes by the teahouse soon. Maybe I'll get up the nerve to talk to him. What if he felt the same way I do but don't know how to come out and express it? He's not like any guy

I've ever seen before. He seems to be sophisticated, cultured, and well rounded. Just the type of guy I would want to have for myself.

I shook myself back into reality. I can't help but wonder what he was doing on this block, where he was going, or even where he was coming from, for that matter. Putting all thoughts of my mystery man aside, I dug into my delicious lunch. I will definitely put this on my list of places to return to. Maybe I can bring my mom by the next time she visits. She loves a good meal and would love the atmosphere.

"Well, gals, it's been good. I guess we'll link up again next week before you each leave me here, right?" I asked as I put my fork on my empty plate.

"Oh, Prue," Connor waved a hand at me. "Don't say it like we're leaving you to die."

"Yeah, you got this girl. You'll figure it out, and we'll both be home before you know it."

"I know, you're right," I sniffed back a tear that threatened to fall, "I'm just going to miss y'all, that's all. Hugs?"

"Of course, girl."

"I love y'all."

"We love you too."

My girls are the best. I didn't expect to get all in my feelings during lunch today. I'm cool. I guess I'm just beginning to feel alone in this big city since I know Connor and Mila will be leaving soon. I know I should be used to it, right. An only child, I should be used to being alone. The truth is, everyone needs companionship. I believe life is better when you're doing it with someone you love. I wish my girls could've stayed longer. Maybe I should have them over next week to stay the night, that way we can stay up and talk all night for old times' sake.

I'm glad Connor and Mila decided to have lunch here in town today. I don't have long to travel back home, especially by myself. I'm not afraid of walking alone or anything, but I'm certainly no fool. You won't catch me out here walking home alone, not after dark for sure. Walking downhill is a lot easier than walking up for sure.

I nearly trip over my shoelace as I am walking. I propped my foot up against a window ledge to tie my shoe. When I put my foot down, I bumped smack into you know who. I couldn't believe it. My heart was pounding inside my chest.

"Oh, I'm sorry, Miss."

I giggled and unfroze my mouth. "Prue, my name is Prudence Palmer, but you can call me Prue."

"Right, I'm sorry, Miss Prue," he apologized with a stunning smile.

"You're good. I really wasn't watching when I got up. What's your name?"

He stuck his hand out, and I placed mine in his. It was warm and inviting. "My name is Jemison James, but you can call me JJ. Where are you headed?"

"Just walking home."

"Oh, word, so am I," he offered me another sexy smile. "Mind if I walk with you?" He fell into step next to me, matching my stride.

"Sure, if you're going this way."

"I am, wait, haven't I seen you before."

I kept a straight face; I didn't want him to think I was thirsty and desperate. "Well, I don't know. Have you ever been to Romans Teahouse?"

"Yeah, I have. It's one of my favorite spots."

I feigned surprise. "Well, I work there. I'm one of the new managers."

"Oh, word. It's become one of my favorite spots," he said as we walked several more blocks in comfortable silence. We stood at the door of my building, and I turned to walk up the steps.

"Well, here's my stop. Maybe I'll see you around."

"Most definitely, take it easy."

"Yeah, you do the same."

I opened the building's door, and once inside, I pumped my fist in the air; I finally know his name! I can't believe we ran, well bumped into each other. This has been quite a day. Wait until I tell my girls. I wonder if he'll be at the house tomorrow.

I ran up to my studio apartment and glanced in my mirror as I sat down my keys. My sweaty, shiny face stared back at me. I need a facial. I guess my mom is going to have to come over sooner rather than later, like ASAP. I'm sure she's ready to install my alarm system, and while she's here, she can clear any dead skin I may have before tomorrow.

I shook my head at my reflection and laughed. What am I doing? I just met this guy. Why am I acting as if we're going to hook up? Well, I don't know what's going to come between Jemison and me, but I must be on my game.

Do not get it twisted. I'm not going to become something I'm not to get him to notice me. I want to present the best version of myself.

Sugar Cane

These last two weeks have really flown by. I guess the saying is true. Time flies when you're having fun. I cannot believe I've said see you later to both of my best friends today. It's like the world stood still.

It's just Jasmine and me from now on. Too bad, she can't talk back. That's what makes her a good listener, though.

I can't believe I haven't seen Jemison in the teahouse since we met three weeks ago. I'm sure he would have taken up space in my mind if I weren't so caught up worrying about my girls. I can't harp on this forever, and I don't plan to.

There's a poetry slam tonight at this restaurant down the block. Of course, I'm not going alone, so I've asked my co-workers Kenny and Stoke, short for Stokeisha, to accompany me. Stoke's name comes from a mixture of Story, Keith, and Eisha. She's a sweet girl with a big name, and trust me. She will correct you every time.

My feelings have been so bottled up lately. I like to think I have the best support system between my mom, great-aunt, and best friends, but I do not tell them all my business. So, I thought, why not compose my feelings into a poem and spill my guts to perfect strangers.

I'm not sure where to begin. All I know is my feelings are in a tailspin. I pulled the sticky notes from my journal to see if I can find some inspiration to tie all my feelings together to compose something. I refuse to get caught up in the what-ifs. It's better to get it out now to save me the heartache later.

At least I have the teahouse. I will rather be swept away by the sweet aroma and the lives of my many guests and what they're up to in their own lives. I need to focus. Let me burn some incense and play some jams. Maybe then the words of how I'm feeling will finally come together. Let me at least try to compose something.

Here goes...

You're there
I'm here
Although I'm afraid, there's nothing to fear.
What do you suppose I do?
Figuring it all out is all that I ever do.
I'm content but somehow ready for something new.
Truth is, I miss y'all and hope that you miss me too.

Wow, I guess that's it. Who knew that all my emotions would turn me into a poet? First time for everything, I guess. That seems to be the motto this year. All this newness is becoming a bit complicated, but I suppose that's because I let it. I should get over the fact that my girls and I have all chosen different paths. Despite my lack of planning, I still believe that this path chose me.

Why am I suddenly so worried about what's to be? I love a

good mystery. I guess the only thing for me to do is brew myself a nice cup of tea. By the time I reach the bottom of the cup, I'm sure my soul will appreciate the realness of myself.

I went through my tea cabinet, pulling out different tea sachets and bags. I settled on a simple mixture of green tea with sugar. Sometimes simplicity makes all the difference.

Have you ever felt hostage inside of your own mind? It's like the only thing to free myself right now is writing it all out and sipping the savory tea. It's as if I wrote out all my feelings onto tea leaves with an edible pen and brewed them. It's like me swallowing my feelings, my pride, the fact that I say I'm fine, but I know all these changes I've been going through is just going to take some time.

Anyway, the past is behind me, and the future lies ahead with doors just waiting to be opened. I'm not sure when Mila would be home again, but I'm sure I'll see Connor during the holidays. I can always keep up with them through Facetime and Instagram. I hope Mila can use IG in the military.

I've been so lost in my thoughts that my tea is ready. Anywho, my tea is finally a brew, bottoms up. By the time I reach the bottom of this cup, I'm sure my mind will no longer be running amuck. I need to be off to work so that we can all leave on time for the poetry slam tonight.

The melodies of the teahouse pulled me out of the puddle of the slum of my feelings. I glanced around at the customers sipping their favorite brews. There are a few new faces in the house today. I love figuring out their stories, but I also love picking up where I left off with the regulars.

The bell over the door rang, and I glanced up, heart skipping a beat. The man's smooth sailing as if his feet don't even touch the floor when he walks. It's like he floats on air. You guessed it. It's Mister Jemison James himself.

"Well, hello, Miss, manager."

"Mr. James," I replied as if we're on a formal level with one another.

If you don't know me by now, then stop and brew you another cup of tea.

You know I have to play it cool despite the beads of sweat that's rolling off of me. Oh my, my, my. Why is this boy so fine? I could probably do a lot better with keeping my composure if he weren't so easy on the eyes. I need to get it together, but I can't stop grinning.

"So, what you've been up to," he asked, leaning against the counter bar.

I started to wipe down the counters. "You're looking at it, but you know I could ask you the same thing."

"I just been working," he shrugged. "You know how that is, I'm sure."

"Good for you. What would you like today?"

"Well, I was thinking, why don't you surprise me?"

I grinned and gestured behind me. "Okay, cool. Tell you what, why don't you choose a cup size and I'll go ahead and ring you up."

"Alright, bet. I'm sure it's going to be good."

I nearly floated through the doors and into the kitchen. Stoke grinned at me.

"Prue, who is that?" She batted her eyes toward the bar.

"Oh, that's Jemison. He's been coming here for a few weeks now." I tried to play it cool but lost. "And before you ask, yes, dibs. I'm not even going to front as if I don't find him attractive."

"Girl, I'm glad you did because I was sure going to spark up a conversation when I go to clean up that table."

"You are a mess. I never met girls who were so direct."

"Well, in this day and age, you have to shoot your shot right."

Stoke had a point. What if I shoot my shot and miss? But you never know unless you try. It's not like I'm trying to marry the guy. We barely know each other.

Like really, Jemison is very easy on the eyes, but I wonder what I'm missing. I guess I'll just put that question on the back burner and get to know him first. I don't want to do things between the lines. I want to flirt and be flirted with. I want to engage in conversation that leaves him wanting more and long to discover just who I am. I'm done with being afraid and filling my mind with worry and what-ifs. Let's do this.

I walked back to the bar area, putting a little extra in my step. "Hey Jemison, here's your tea. I hope you like it. You know what, I know you're going to like it."

"Okay, I never doubted you," he took a sip, paused, then smiled. "Oh Prue, this is good. There's a hint of something in here, but I just can't put my finger on it."

I grinned. "I call it the blackberry psalmist. It's a blackberry blend with a hint of lemon, honey, and vanilla."

He snapped his fingers. "That's it, vanilla. This is pretty good. This just made it to my new top three. Thanks, Prue," he took another sip, longer this time holding my eyes.

"Anytime, Jemison."

"You know you can call me JJ, right?"

"Yea, I know. I'll see you later, JJ." I turned to leave to grab another cup for one of the regulars who sat and signaled me to come over.

JJ touched my arm, making me pause and look down. "Hey,

what are you doing tonight?"

"Well, my coworkers and I are going to a poetry slam. What about you?"

"That's crazy because I'm going to a poetry slam as well. I was going to see if you wanted to join me."

My heart skipped several beats, but I kept my cool. "Well, I guess I'll see you there."

"I guess so. Thanks again for the tea," JJ stood, offered me a crooked smile, and placed some money under the cup.

"Don't mention it. Enjoy."

What are the odds, right? When I've soaked in my feelings all day about my friends leaving, here comes mister suave to come in and jack up my feelings again. My goodness, it's like I can't catch a break today. I'm going, to be honest, though, I'm glad he came today. Jemison walking in here gave me chills and sweats all at the same time. It's crazy. What are the odds that he came through today on all days and that he's even going to be at the poetry slam tonight? Like really, why is he all up in my groove. But again, if I'm honest, baby is a whole mood. AHHHH, what am I doing? I can't stop grinning, and every time I looked up, his eyes were locking with mine.

"Hey, you guys, I'll be right back," I called through the kitchen. "I need to run to the restroom."

"Okay, we got it, girl," Stoke said, coming through the door. "Take your time, no rush."

Whew child! This is one reason I'm glad I don't wear base. I splashed my face a few times. *Just breathe, Prue, get it together, girl. I mean, he's nice-looking, but this boy is not that fine, like calm down girl.* Uh, I feel like I'm going to be sick. My stomach is literally quivering, and I can't stop shaking. *What is this boy doing to me?* If I'm acting like this now, how in the heck am I going to see him tonight, let alone reading my poem in front of him?

I was cool at first when I didn't think he was interested. How in the world did I allow myself to become so smitten like what the heck, get yourself together, Prudence. Man, I'm starting to sound like my mom when she has something serious to tell me.

I took a deep breath. Well, at least I can work in peace now without my heart pounding as if it's going to burst right out of my chest. I'll have some peppermint tea; mint always seems to keep me calm. I guess it's nature's way of soothing you from the inside out.

Watching JJ walk through that teahouse door was just what I needed to turn my frown upside down. He's pretty suave, but who knew he would also be pretty sweet. Let's be real, though, what was him allowing me to choose his tea all about. It's like he's placing the ball in my court to shoot my shot. Well, he can forget it.

Call me crazy, but I'm looking forward to seeing how JJ plans to shoot his shot. Why else would he take such an initiative to show me that he trusts my judgment in selecting his drink? Oh, no! What have I done? Now I can't even remember what he normally drinks. I have to figure it out. Why am I so blinded by the steam that I can't even see, let alone think clearly? I have to get it together and fast.

Mint

Now, this is good. I can't remember the last time I've had peppermint tea. I'm just glad to feel calm again. I might as well figure out what I'm wearing tonight.

I glanced at my wardrobe. Hmm, I think I'll keep it simple as usual—earth tones with a bit of chill and street. Just because I live in Manhattan now does not mean that I can't continue to dress comfortably like me and my homies in Brooklyn. I think I'll wear my white tube top with khaki cargo joggers and my all-white Adidas would be a nice touch.

I sat on the balcony with Jasmine and burned some incense. Something about the smell sweeps me off my feet into a realm of peace and serenity. I guess I'm used to smelling them from going to yoga each week.

Roman lives by incense for sure. He says, "It's a gateway to open the unknown of the ultimate possibilities of what could be, let your mind wander." Mom and I use to laugh at him, but now I'm starting to think he's onto something. I'm still trying to figure out where this life of mine is going to take me. There's a world of possibilities just waiting to be discovered. I'm starting to question whether I'm cut out for this life of discovery…

I shook the incense out and left the balcony. I couldn't wait to get to the coffee shop. That's where the poetry slam is tonight.

My intercom rang.

"What's good?"

"Yo, homegirl, let's go," Kenny and Stoke said at the same time.

"Alright, grabbing my satchel and heading right down."

Kenny and Stoke are a whole vibe. I'm so thankful to have met them by working at the teahouse. Stoke is my age, eighteen, and Kenny's twenty-one. He's like the big brother I've always wanted. Like he's super cool. He doesn't hit on us or anything. It's hard to have guy friends. These fools always want something from you, and you know what I mean.

I didn't date a whole lot in high school. I didn't want to date the egotistic, thuggish wannabes like every other girl in my class. Those chicks always ended up dating the same ole guys anyway. It never ended well. As soon as the girls fell out with each other, they started dating each other's man. Like how does, 'I'll take your dude' became the best revenge. I think it's stupid and completely nasty if you ask me. Like who does that other than THOTs? Those girls weren't truly friends, if you ask me. Not like Connor, Mila, and me. We would never do each other like that.

We walked into an adorable coffee shop. Very classic, a lot like the one my mom and I would often go to back in Brooklyn. I headed over to the counter.

"Hey, I'm Prue," I told the barista. "I'm doing spoken word tonight."

"Great, you're number four," she says.

Surprisingly, I'm not nervous at all. As I scan the room, I

don't see JJ anywhere. It's a blessing in disguise because I definitely do not want to revisit the quivering stomach situation I experienced earlier. No one has time for any of that. You feel me.

A handsome woman with several tattoos came up to the mic. "Alright, babes and lames, nawl y'all alright with me. Coming to the stage is a woman with caution, miss Prue Palmer. Please give her a hand and be nice. This is her first night. Let's treat her right."

I jumped up and made my way to the mic. I smiled at my friends before I read. "This one goes out to everyone just trying to figure it out in a world where they may feel alone."

You're there
I'm here
Although I'm afraid, there's nothing to fear.
What do you suppose I do?
Figuring it all out is all that I ever do.
I'm content but somehow ready for something new.
Truth is, I miss y'all and hope that you miss me too.

"Give it up for Miss Prue Palmer! Alright, girl, you have to come back. We are here for you. You got friends right here at the *Nine to Five*," the poetry MC announced as I went back to my chair to thunderous applause. "Alright, coming next to the stage is number five. I guess like Good Times, this brother is dynamite. Please give it up for one of my homies Jemison James, Mister JJ himself people."

WHAT?!?! I couldn't believe it. Coming from the back of the coffee house was JJ. My stomach is beginning to sink. I can't believe he's been in the room this entire time, hearing me spill my lonely guts. I can't turn back now. I might as well enjoy a caramel macchiato and see what this brother has to say.

JJ stood up there, looking fine in the spotlight. "Thank you, everyone! To my boy Skillz, thanks for making me do this man, You're a real one."

She wears her hair in a bun.
I don't even know her name.
I think she's fly and curious.
Some say she's plain Jane.
The difference between them and me; we're just not the same.
Call me lame, but I want to know more than her name.
Learn of her sweet ambiance
And the way she fights off the vultures.
You see, this girl is pretty fly.
The brightest of young ladies that make me wish to touch the sky
This girl got me Hella high.
From the steam of her cup
I wish to take her home and drink her up.
Don't get me wrong
I want to introduce her to momma.
Sip on her thoughts
And relieve her of the drama.

I jumped and spilled my macchiato on my lap. "Ouch!"

"Prue, you good?" asked Kenny

"Yeah, I'm good," I said, grabbing a bunch of napkins from the table.

I couldn't believe it. Call me crazy, but you can't deny the fact that it sounds like JJ was describing me in his poem. Butterflies danced in my stomach. This boy has me wide open. How did this happen? Where did he even come from? We've barely shared more than a few exchanges. I've never felt this way before. I don't think I want to let it go either. I can't deny it, JJ just slam-dunk. I wanted him to shoot his shot. I guess it's like Maya Angelo said, "Ask for what you want and be prepared to get it."

The butterflies turned into a tornado as JJ joined us at the table. I tried to keep myself from grinning.

"Hey, stranger. How are you?" JJ asked as he slid into the seat next to me. Kenny and Stoke had gotten up to grab more coffee and grinned at me from the bar.

"I'm good. How are you? Your poem was dope."

"Yeah, yours too. Look, Prue, I wanted to ask you here tonight because I wanted you to hear it. Look, since the first time I came to the tea house, I wanted to get to know you."

I felt my cheeks heat up. "Oh wow, JJ, I'm flattered."

"Before you say no, just let me take you out on Thursday."

"JJ, I wasn't going to say no. I would like that a lot."

"Oh, word, it's a date then."

"Yeah, cool, let me give you my number. Text me, and I'll give you my address."

"Sounds good. I'm headed to get a bite from the counter. Can I get you a penne or something?"

"Sure, I'll like the "grilled tomato, chevre, and thyme baguette sandwich."

Kenny and Stoke chose that moment to return to the table with coffee and pastries. "You got it, wait, who's your friends?"

"This is Kenny and Stoke."

"Hey, I'm Jemison. You can call me…"

"We know, JJ, nice word, man."

"Yeah, it was alright."

"Thanks," JJ looked at me. "I will be right back."

Stoke slid into the chair and leaned forward." Dang girl, he is all that."

I giggled. "I know, right, oh my goodness. We're going out on Thursday."

"Oh, sweet! I bet he's going to take you somewhere Hella nice!" Stoke exclaimed.

"We shall see, won't we?"

I am at a loss for words. I can't believe JJ was going to ask me here so that I could hear the poem he wrote about me. I am in total awe that he would even do something like that. I mean, it's risky. What if I weren't interested? I could have seriously dissed him like other girls who are uninterested when guys approach them. Here we are. I guess the feelings mutual.

The jazzy beat of the coffee shop fades away, and everyone in the room seems to disappear. It's like JJ, and I are the only ones left standing here. Face to face, looking eye to eye as if we're daring to venture through the souls of one another's whole life as we both enter into a realm of wonder. Ironically, he kind of feels familiar. Like a gentle spirit that's always been right there, waiting in my shadows.

Swept away in this dreamlike reality. I finally got a good thing for me. I was good with myself and didn't need anyone else. Having him, though, is starting to make my life a little sweeter.

I feel like I'm dreaming, but I'm very much awake. I don't understand the words that are flowing from JJ. I bet I look pretty stupid sitting here casually nodding to whatever it is he's saying. I wish I could be present without my mind spiraling out of control. I have got to get a freaking grip.

"I'm sorry, JJ. What were you saying?"

He paused. "Oh, I'm sorry, is the music too loud. We can go outside."

"Yeah, let's do that," I followed him through the door and into the night air. It seemed to shock my mind awake.

"Better?"

"Yeah, much better," I sighed. "What were you saying?"

He leaned against the graffiti-covered wall. "I was saying that the last guy was pretty dope."

"Yeah, he was cool."

He smiled again and almost looked shy. "What are you getting into this week."

"Work mostly," I shrugged. "I'm never too sure. I guess wherever the wind takes me."

"See, that's why you're so interesting Prue, you're such a free spirit. I wish I were more like that."

Just then, Kenny and Stoke came out. Both had worried looks on their faces for a hot second. "Hey Prue, you ready to go?" Kenny asked. "We're about to head out."

"Yeah, we can go."

JJ pushed himself off the wall. "I guess this is good night then. I look forward to seeing you Thursday, so I'm going to say later."

"I like that, later then."

Bliss

Talk about a great night. I'm so glad I didn't chicken out of going to a poetry night at the coffee shop. I could have really missed out on a wonderful time.

Anyway, it's HUMP DAY! I'm so ready to free myself of all these emotional world winds and find some Zen alongside my mom and Roman.

"Good afternoon, Mrs. Judy!" I said as I placed a teapot and one of our more exotic teacups in front of her.

"Hiya, beauty. Can you spare an old lady a moment of your time?"

"Sure, how are you?" I said, sitting down across from her. "Are you enjoying your tea?"

"Always, dear. I just wanted to chat with you for a spell."

"Yes, ma'am."

"I've noticed a change in you lately," she patted me maternally on the hand. "You're smiling from ear to ear, with a brighter twinkle in your eye."

"Oh, Mrs. Judy. I'm just happy, that's all."

She laughed, sounding like tinkling bells. "Oh, don't I know it, dear. I've been seeing that young man in here and the way you began to shine brighter than the sun."

"Mrs. Judy," I started to say, a little embarrassed.

"Don't worry, my love, it's not that obvious. I know you well enough to know when something different or when my tea is a little sweeter, you know," Mrs. Judy sipped her tea. "I want to encourage you to love, even if it's for a little while. The greatest life lessons are often brought through the most unexpected seasons. "

"Yes, ma'am."

"I don't want you to overthink, dearie. I was your age once, you know. I want you to enjoy your life no matter what each new day brings."

"Yes, ma'am, thanks, Mrs. Judy," the door to the shop opened, and I stood to greet another customer.

"Any time, dear. And Prue?"

"Yes, ma'am?" I paused for a moment.

"Find joy not only in the tea you drink but in the people you meet."

I grinned. "Yes, ma'am, I'll keep that in mind."

Mrs. Judy is such a doll. She's like the grandmother I'd wish I had grown up with. My mom would call her a nosey old bat for meddling in her business. Good thing I'm not like my mother in that aspect. I may not always agree with people, but I'm always opened to hear what they have to say, whether I choose to take heed or not. I'm thankful for Mrs. Judy. She seems to know more about me than I gave her credit for. Here I am studying the regulars in the house as if they were my personal guests to discover that they were getting to know me too.

The house is packed today. The autumn crisp air is beginning to roll in, and people can't resist some of our best seasonal favorites. I am personally excited to use crisp apples that we add to just about every pastry and a few teas to provide our guests with the sweet taste of apple cider tea to quench their thirst.

I absolutely love the fall season. Sure, it may be a little nippy out, but that's what a cute scarf and a warm cup of tea are for. I'm usually a lot happier during this time of year. I guess it's the smiles on everyone's face when they take their first sip of tea to warm up from the chilly outdoors. I love making people happy.

I guess I've been on a peppermint high for the last few weeks. I've been making all kinds of variations of peppermint tea. If you name it, I've tried it. It's so soothing and relaxing. I needed it and found it too good to keep to myself.

I glanced at the clock on the wall. It's almost time for yoga. This early afternoon rush just flew right past me. My mom is running late as usual. I'm sure she ran into a top-dollar buyer who wants to buy one of her new sculptures. I can't say that I blame her. If anyone is out here collecting their coins while doing what they love, it's my mom.

Sage

"Uh, Roman does it again," Mom sighed and stretched as we left Roman's studio.

"I so needed that," I agreed.

"Me too, Puss. How about we go and grab a bite to eat?"

"Yeah, let's," I thought for a hot second. "I know just the spot."

I walked Mom down to the Mediterranean restaurant and took a seat by the window, just like I did with Connor and Mila.

"Oh, Prue," Mom said with a mouthful of food. "This has got to be the best Mediterranean food I've ever had."

"I know, right. I said you would like it."

Mom took a sip of water. "So how are you adjusting since the girls left?"

I shrugged and toyed with my fork. "It was tough at first for sure. I wasn't sure that I was able to deal at first. I guess I was really in my head about them leaving me. It felt like...like."

"Abandonment?"

"Yeah, I guess it does. But on a more positive note, I'm very thankful for Kenny and Stoke. Kenny's like a big brother, and

Stoke is my ace boon coon. I guess because she reminds me so much of Connor."

Mom nearly spat out her water. "Oh, Lord. You must mean she can eat."

"Momma, through a house and a home," I laughed. "I don't get it. She's toothpick thin, like where is she putting it all."

"It's a gift, I guess."

I rolled my eyes. "Yeah, coming from another toothpick, only you are like Coca-Cola bottle thick."

"Hey," Mom smacked my hand. "Watch it, girl, momma is the meal."

"A snack, ma, a snack," I rolled my eyes. "I told you no one says meal—uh."

"Righhht. Anyway, anything else new?"

"Well, I did meet a guy," I said, shrinking down into my seat.

"Oh, really. That's a change of pace."

"I know. Mom, he's so great."

"Okay, well, what is Mr. Great's name?"

"Sorry, his name is Jemison James. He goes by JJ."

"Jemison James, that's a strong name."

"Yeah, he's fit for sure. He's tall and thin but has a muscular build."

Mom got a weird look on her face. "Jemison James, I don't know why his name is ringing a bell."

I sighed. "Oh, here we go. Please don't tell me he's some long-lost relative or worse, my half-brother."

"No, no, nothing like that. I'm not sure where I've heard his name before, but it definitely sounds familiar. Anyway, I'm happy for you, suh."

"Oh, Mom. I don't even say that. Just let that one go."

"Yeah, maybe you're right. Anyways, I have to get back, dear.

This was nice. I'll definitely be coming back to eat here. Call me when you get home?" She got up and started getting her things. I stood up and hugged her.

"Of course. Steak."

"Shake—love you, babe."

My mom is everything. Sure, she may be corny, but everything she does and says has so much meaning. She always says *God doesn't waste resources, so why should we.* Ever since I can remember, we've always departed from one another by saying steak and shake. Mom says that steaks resemble fine dining and shakes are for unwinding. Either way, it's nice to have them become a part of your personal routine, she would always say. I guess it's sort of like how we go to yoga every Wednesday to rejuvenate.

I wish she didn't have to runoff. I didn't even get a chance to tell her that JJ and I have a date planned for tomorrow. It's probably for the best. My mom gives good advice, but she can be old school and out of touch. Baby is a trip. I love her, though.

I started to hurry down the street a little. I'm sure Kenny and Stoke are arguing over the register drawer. They do this every Wednesday when I leave for break. We're all cool, but those two fight like an old married couple who absolutely hate each other. The two of them have a love-hate relationship, and they don't even try to hide, let alone deny it. I try to keep them separate when we're all scheduled to work together, which is rare.

Roman said it's bad for business the way those two carry on. Trust me. Roman is not the one to get on his bad side. Once you disrupt his ying and yang, you can kiss his Zen goodbye.

The teahouse was empty for a Wednesday. The yogi's usually staying for lunch after the yoga session must be going to an event somewhere nearby, I suppose.

"I don't believe my eyes," I said to Kenny and Stoke. "I just knew you two would be up here going off on each other."

"Girl, please," Stoke reprimanded. Roman came down here talking about his Zen and us disrupting his equilibrium with all our bickering, whatever that means."

"I knew it was too good to be true," I laughed as I patted Kenny on the back as I walked past.

Stoke must have really upset Kenny because he hadn't said one word the rest of the afternoon. I mean, we barely even looked at one another. I wonder what Stoke said that really set him off-kilter. Don't get me wrong, the two of them fight like this all the time, but usually, they start talking to each other within minutes. Stoke had to have really gotten under his skin.

"Hey, Mr. Tom, how are you?" I asked, setting down a plate of chocolate chip cookies.

"Doing just fine, Prue, just fine. What about you?"

"Never better, if I were any better, I would be you. You're always in such good spirits."

He waved a cookie at me. "Well, when you get to be my age, there's no sense in frowning. Times a ticking. I rather make up for all my wrongs in my youth instead of parading around like some old crazy coot."

I laughed. "Not sure what you mean, Mr. Tom, but I'll take your word for it. I hope you enjoy the rest of your tea."

"I always do, thanks to you."

"Aww, that's sweet, thanks, Mr. Tom."

The tension in this room is so thick that you can slice it with a knife. I try to stick to my "no tea policy." I know you think I'm totally tripping, but I'm talking about figuratively. I try to tend to my own business unless it's strictly on a need-to-know basis to better others. I think the wounds between Kenny and

Sage

Stoke are still too fresh.

If I'm honest, though, it's a whole mood in here, and they are really killing my vibes, and I'm sure our guests are suffering too. There's only one thing left to do. Instead of involving Roman, I'm just going to burn some sage and clear this room of all its negative vibes.

Before you come for me, no, I am not a witch. Respect the culture. It's been practiced by many to rid places of negative energies. I like to protect my positive energy as much as possible.

After a few minutes of sage burning, it's starting to feel better in here already. Maybe I should mix them up a special brew and drop a few fresh pieces of sage. Once they take one sip from their cups, I'm sure it'll cheer them both up. Nothing says peace like a little sage.

I handed both of them a teacup and waited. Sure enough, they started smiling at each other.

"Thanks, Prue, you always know just what to do—well, brew, in this case," Stoke said.

"Don't mention it. I want you guys to be good. I love you both, and since this place was made for relaxing don't you guys think, maybe you should, I don't know—relax."

"Yeah, Prue, you're right."

"I'm sorry, Kenny."

"Yeah—me too. Don't mention it. Come here, girl," Kenny pulled Stoke in for a tight hug.

"Boy, stop—you are stupid."

"I'm glad everything is straight, for now at least," I tell them.

Yoga definitely did me some good. Plus, having lunch with mom was the honey to my tea—ha-ha. Whew, child, I cracked my own self up with that one.

Feeling thirsty? Need a refill? This may be the perfect time to brew yourself another cup. Yes, I'm talking to you. Make it quick.

The bell over the door jingled, and I glanced up. A strange man is heading towards the counter, and something tells me that he's about to spice things up. I stood near the spice rack. By the look of his newspaper tucked under his arm and the large laptop case, it looks like he'll be here awhile. I'm glad Stoke is already near the register. This gives me a chance to really study this newbie.

I mean, it's not uncommon to have never seen him before. We have people that come in here for the very first time daily. Something about him has spiked my curiosity, though. Not like Jemison. This is a different kind of fascination. I don't want to date this man. I'm not even physically attracted to him. But for some odd reason, I'm drawn in with his every subtle movement.

The short, Asian man spoke in clips, which got my curiosity running.

"Hey, Stoke, what did tiny order," I whispered to her as I lean with my back against the counter, trying not to be so obvious. "He just asked for a green tea with nothing added," Stoke whispered back to me. Hmm, this is a tough one.

I have never encountered someone who just merely wanted green tea without having anything added to it. No sugar, no spice, nor honey. I find it quite strange. I've never met anyone that didn't take anything with their tea. I mean, it's tea. It isn't enjoyable without adding a little something, something to it. I personally like to add sugar, honey, or sugar and honey. It really depends on the kind of tea I'm drinking that day and what I'm in the mood for.

Sage

I wonder what he's like outside of here. He seems to be a man of few words. I wonder why. Maybe he speaks broken English and is rarely understood. Who knows…I wonder if Roman has ever seen him before? Too bad he ran off to a lunch date of his own after yoga.

I'm not quite sure why I'm so obsessed with this man. I must look like a totally starker lunatic the way I keep glancing over at him. I need to do something. I know, I can wash the windows and tidy up all the sitting areas. That stuff always needs to be done.

"Hi, how are you?" I said to the man as I walk by.

"Hello," he replied without asking how I am doing in return. See what I mean, a man of little words. He appears to be very ordinary. But there's definitely something there. He's getting up to leave now. I sure hope he comes back.

Butterscotch

I can't believe that Thursday is finally here. This week has gone by very slowly.

I have nothing to wear. I mean, I have something to wear, but I don't know—WHAT I'm going to wear. I don't even know where we're going or what Jemison has planned. He's so unpredictable. By the tea he drinks, I figured he was, you know—the good guy type. Thankfully, I was right. It's a beautiful thing when your wants come to fruition. You feel me.

I would have felt like a complete goober had Jemison not liked me back. The feeling is mutual, and I'm glad. There's nothing better than liking somebody than when that person likes you too. Being yourself always goes a long way. It beats putting on some wack charade that you'll have to keep up until one day you finally break from all the fakery.

I want my outfit to say, *hey, aren't I the most beautiful thing you've ever seen?* But I don't want it to say, *let's quit the small talk, let's Netflix and chill.* I don't know about you, but I refuse to deliver my cookies to just anybody because they showed me some attention. I'm more than just some cookie that you can snack on whenever your sweet tooth gets a craving, you know. On top of that, I'm a lady.

Anyway, back to my wardrobe dilemma, my outfit has to be just right. You see, my outfit at the poetry slam was fitting for chilling with the crew and giving a vibe as I delivered my word to the people. This is different. This sets the tone of who I am and what JJ will expect when seeing me.

Let's see. I can always go in a dress and a blue jean jacket. You can't go wrong with that. Besides, I don't want to text him and say, *"Hey, where are we going so that I know what to wear."* I don't know. That seems a little extra and superficial, which I am not. I'll play it safe by wearing a dress to stay cool.

Thick thighs may save lives, or so they say. In my case, thick thighs sweat especially if I forget to put on Vaseline to avoid chaffing. That's the price you pay for being "thick," though. Never know what you're going to get with genetics. Isn't it crazy how we girls over analyze everything?

Great! It's almost one. I guess I'll just be doing a wash and go today. At least, I won't be wearing a bun, that's for sure. I can't help but wonder if JJ is at home sweating bullets just as I am. I wonder if he lives alone, too or if he has roommates. I'm really looking forward to learning more about him. Anywho, I guess I can wear a little eyeliner and mascara today. I might as well jazz it up a bit if I'm going to go through the trouble of wearing a dress to God knows where.

Whew, Child… look at me. Nervous than a jaywalker with three strikes. I inhaled a deep breath and exhaled it out slowly; I'm just going to chill. This boy has seen me with my hair in a messy bun in an apron with khakis.

Everything that I am is amazing. I'm authentic, nerdy, and a foodie. If, for some reason, that's not enough for Jemison, then he's not the one for me. I don't believe in wasting my time.

I'm not saying that this date is a waste of time but that I value my time and other's time. If I'm sharing my moments with you, then you must be pretty special. In turn, I hope that person feels the same. You see, this is why I don't like casually dating. I'm already getting too involved and jumping the gun. How do people do this? Like how do you go out with somebody you like and not sweat it? I got it. Maybe I should treat JJ like the homie. That way, there are no strings attached if this thing goes left.

Ring, ring.

I kept my voice steady. "Hello, you've ringed Prue."

"Hey Prue, it's JJ. You ready to go?"

"Hey, yes. I'll be right down."

I fanned myself with my hand. "Whew, sweet baby Jesus. Lord, please give me peace as I go on this date. In Jesus name, Amen."

Is it me, or did my staircase get longer? JJ stood at the bottom of the staircase so suave. Like, there is no other word to really describe the very essence of his being. Looks aren't everything, but God has made some beautiful people. His looks are just a bonus. His kindness surpasses his looks any day and really what makes him so beautiful. It's his spirit.

"Hey, you," I said as I stepped down.

"Hey Prue, how are you?" he says as he moves towards me for a hug.

Whew, Lord. This is going to be harder than I thought. He smells so good; he's wearing Polo Black. That is like a guy's ultimate signature of "girl come here." Nope. I can't allow myself to be trapped by that. I side hugged him so quick you would have sworn we were greeting each other at church.

"So, where are we going?" I ask as we began walking down the sidewalk.

"Well, I thought we would stop to grab a drink first," he said as he stuck his hands in his back pockets. "I know a cool spot that has a different twist on tea. It just opened, so I thought it would be cool to check it out together."

"Oh, okay, great. You know I love tea."

"Yea, I gathered. I like tea too. I like to think of myself as a bit of a tea enthusiast."

"Aaayee, that's dope. I like that. A tea enthusiast. It's so nice out today."

I tried to contain my beating heart. "Yeah, it is. I love our city just for that reason. The beauty of walking everywhere and enjoying what the earth has to offer."

"Huh, that's one way to look at it. I guess I never thought about it like that before." He reached for my hand. Oddly enough, it has calmed my nerves.

JJ is sweet as ever, and he's so insightful. I like to listen to his outlook on simple things. I like that we both have a thing for tea. I guess that's the commonality that brought us together in the first place.

Holding hands as we walk to this new tea spot is everything. It feels so right. I enjoy the easiness of it all. JJ is so easy going and a joy to talk to. I could listen to him for hours. I like the way his mouth curls to the side when he grins. Silly, I know, but it's the little things that always draw my attention.

"Well, here we are," JJ said as he lets go of my hand to open the door.

I have never heard of Boba Tea before. After we ordered, we talked to the owner. We were told that Boba pearls are made of tapioca starch from the cassava root, so compassionately that customers can rest easy knowing that gelatin is not used in making these tiny balls of deliciousness. I laugh at the way he says deliciousness like it's the best thing anyone has ever tasted.

I'm impressed that JJ knew about a place like this. It is kind of sweet how he played on the fact that I like tea, being that I work at one of the most popular teahouses in town and all.

"I wonder if this is something Roman would be interested in adding to our menu," I tell JJ as I take a sip of my unicorn flavored boba tea.

"You never know. You might as well give it a shot and ask," he winked at me. I giggled. I'm sure both of my ears are red because I can feel them burning. Luckily, I wore my hair down, so they are covered.

"Come on, let's go," JJ nods to me as he says, "Hey, thanks, man." to the store owner as he holds his cup up.

"Where are we going," I asked him.

"I thought we would go over to the park, get away from all the noise for a bit," he said.

"Okay, okay," I said as I take another sip of my unicorn drink.

As we're getting closer to the park, my stomach is starting to quiver a little bit. I've been in Manhattan for a while now and have never visited Central Park. I'm not sure if these are nerves or if I'm excited to finally getting to go. Roman has told me that it's pretty nice. He walks there often.

"Well, that was pretty good," I tell JJ as we throw our cups away. "Oh cool, they have recycling bins. Let's empty the boba beads and put our cups in here."

"Oh, so you're a go green fan, huh," JJ asked as he puts his cup in the bin.

"Yeah, I try to do my part."

"That's pretty cool, Prue. I can definitely do better in that area," he said as he rubs the back of his head.

We walk around the park for a bit. I love how quiet it is out there. People aren't even allowed to ride their bikes in certain areas of the park. It's so peaceful.

"We should get going before it gets too late. There's one more place I want to take you," he said as he grabbed my hand. I love that JJ is so sure of himself and takes the lead as a man should.

A thought popped out of my mouth. "Hey JJ, how old are you?

"I guess we never did exchange that information, did we. I'm twenty-two. How old are you?"

"I just turned nineteen a month or so ago."

He laughed. "Oh word, you are so mature for your age."

I shrugged. "Yeah, I get that a lot. People say it seems like I'm way before my time like I've been here before."

We walked a couple of more blocks. Then he stopped in front of a door with a picture of animals on it.

"What are we doing here?" I asked as he opened the door for me.

"What, you don't like animals?"

"I do, but I have just never randomly gone to an animal shelter." "Come on, Prue, it'll be fun," he grinned at me as we walked in. An animal shelter. I'm not high maintenance or anything, but I've never envisioned going to an animal shelter for a first date. I'm lowkey embarrassed and feel stupid for not asking Jemison what he had planned so that I could have dressed accordingly. I might as well make the best of it. I'm just not sure what we're doing here. Like, is he planning to adopt a dog or something?

It's so sad here. Kid you not, it feels like one of those ASPCA commercials. All I can hear in my head is the jingle for it as I walk through this building.

"Aww, man, Prue, look at this one," JJ pointed.

"Awe, he's so cute. What's his name?" I ask the lady working the shelter.

The woman looked over her files. "Well, this brown Labradoodle's name is Butterscotch. Isn't he precious? He's sweet like sugar, poor thing. A guy found him tied to a dumpster in an alleyway. People are so cruel just leaving him there like that. Good thing he was brought in. I'm sure someone will adopt him."

"Do you mind if we take him to the play yard and play with him?" JJ asked as he kneeled to allow Butterscotch to smell his hand.

The woman smiled. "Sure, I know he'll enjoy the company. Let me grab his leash."

I'm not going to lie. I'm starting to itch just thinking about fleas. I'm sure these dogs have been treated, though. Shelters are good like that. I'm trying really hard to control my facial expression.

Oh goodness, Butterscotch is headed straight towards me. Oh no, oh no, oh no.

"Hi puppy, please don't bite me," I giggled nervously.

"Come on, Prue, don't you want to pet him. You know they say a dog is a man's best friend."

"Right, a man's not a woman's," I muttered under my breath.

"Awe, Prue, come on, he's harmless."

Butterscotch is rubbing against my leg with his curly soft fur. I can't believe it. This pup has melted my heart. Just look at those big eyes and that wet button nose. Wow, he's as smooth as JJ. I'm in love. I want to cuddle him up and take him home, the dog that is. Don't go getting any ideas.

I reached down and stroked the dog behind the ears. "JJ, this dog is so sweet and very cute, I may add."

"He is, isn't he," JJ waved around the room. "I come here at least once a week to walk and bathe the dogs. I hate the fact that they're just abandoned here."

"JJ, that's so sweet."

"I hope Butterscotch finds a family soon."

"Yeah, me too. Who knows, he may already have."

Gingerly

My date with Jemison was everything. I can't believe I was fretting over an outfit when there are homeless dogs in the city. I couldn't imagine not having Jasmine in my life. People are so cruel to animals. They should really be ashamed of themselves.

On the other hand, though, I wonder what situation they must have been in to have a pet, then turn around and abandon it. It's a sad reality, the world we live in. JJ showed me that he's in tune with his sensitive side for sure.

As JJ and I spoke on the phone this past week, I finally discovered what it is that he does. JJ is a big-time marketing rep at one of the largest firms right here in Manhattan. I'm glad to know that he's close, you know. Oh yeah, all that talk about him being a tea enthusiast was him being modest for sure. JJ is getting ready to study to become a tea sommelier.

Basically, it's a professional tea steward. With the certification, he'll be able to pull in big bucks and work for high-end events and even own a teahouse of his own. The possibilities are endless. JJ knows more about tea than I do. No wonder he's always hanging around and finishing up work at the teahouse. It's like killing two birds with one stone, I guess.

Oh, JJ thinks I should pursue becoming a tea sommelier as well. I told him I would at least think about it. I mean, I just discovered that this was even a thing. Who knew? I sure didn't.

One thing is for certain, even in a season of the unknown, God will never leave you astray. This is when He does His best work. I decided to look it up on the Internet before I made up my mind.

Hmmm…tea sommelier. The program only takes about four weeks or so. That is a major difference from getting a college degree that takes about two to four years, depending on your study program, and this program happens to be online. I never thought about online classes before. This will be a lot of firsts if this turns out to be something that I choose to pursue. It feels right, but I'm really nervous about committing. I should probably look into it more to see how I can use the certification.

The more I thought about it, the more it called to me. I might as well do a service to myself and learn the tea market's ins and outs. I mean, really, where did it all come from? There are tea houses all over the state. Why are they so important to our culture when it was stemmed from somebody else's? I guess that's what connects us as people.

I think I will go through this certification. What can I say? You know I love tea. I love everything about it and how it makes people feel. Especially me. Tea is like the sun on a rainy day. Coming out to cheer you up as you feel the warmth on your face. I know—such a nerd, right. Well, I'll be that. And a good one. No, I'll be the best one. The best tea nerd there is around.

I wonder if sommeliers are on Social Media. I would love to

follow someone's journey. Let's be real. No one wants to go through something completely blindsided. You at least want to know a little bit of what to expect.

When I checked, it looks like mostly white males and only a few women, but no women of color. I wonder why? I guess I'll have to find out.

I wonder if JJ knows anyone who has their sommelier certification. Will he decide to complete the certification online or find somewhere that provides the training. I'm not sure where this path is taking me, but I might as well enjoy the scenery on my way. I can't continue to gingerly creep around things that I'm presented with from fear of failing or messing up. That's never been me. Why am I so afraid now? Tea is already something that sparks my interest. I might as well brace myself, strap in, and take flight.

Who knows, this may actually work for me. I've been flying by the seat of my pants for so long, as my high school counselor use to say. I might as well see if planning could work for me. Yea, I'll sketch out a path, adding things I want to do along the way. It's not like it'll be set in stone. Life happens. It always finds a way to compromise something you wanted to do or a place you wanted to go to.

I want to grab the reins and decide for myself. It's time to change the narrative.

Sommelier

I finally told my mom about me and JJ becoming official and about the two of us pursuing a tea sommelier certification. My mom remembered where she knew JJ from. He was a waiter for one of the art shows she attended downtown. She said that the food paired nicely with each wine.

JJ has been working with the catering business on the side to pay for the tea sommelier certification. His boss taught him about being a sommelier. He knew that JJ likes tea, so he encouraged him to pursue that avenue versus being a traditional sommelier, that and the fact that I don't think he wanted JJ as his competition. Either way, we are now pursuing this journey together—together, I like the sound of that.

It's so refreshing having someone that shares the same interest as me. It's one thing to listen to me rant and rave about things I'm passionate about, but it's totally different when you have someone that gets it. JJ gets me for sure.

As an outgoing introvert, I appreciate JJ for respecting my space when I want to chill alone. Mom says any man that respects boundaries like that is a keeper. I told her that I'd be the judge of that.

I miss my mom. She's been busy working on projects, so she hasn't joined me for yoga on Wednesdays. I still enjoy my time to relax and allow my mind to drift away into a calming orbital world. Instead of the perfect storm, it's my idea of a quiet storm. It's the same feeling I get when it's quietly raining outside, and I can hear the raindrops on my window.

Since I haven't seen my mom much, I've been texting her more often than usual. She's even cornier through text. I was honestly surprised to see her use emojis correctly. Until JJ, my mom is the only person that reminds me who I am when I start to forget and go off on a tangent about what someone else is doing. Not that I'm trying to keep up with the Jones', I just sometimes get swept away by my own insecurities because of all the things I see Connor and Mila post on social media. We're all still cool. However, we don't talk as often as we use to.

On a happier, non-sappy note, JJ and I will be going over the required courses to take for our sommelier certification. I have all the feels today—Issa mood. I mean, of course, I'm excited to get to spend time with JJ, but I'm more excited about starting this new tea venture.

Roman has been very encouraging. He said that once I begin my courses, he would quiz me on tea while at work. I'm so glad that he's such a cool boss and a great support system for me through all of this.

My phone is flashing. That's probably JJ saying when he's coming by. He is probably leaving the animal shelter. I've even started going with him sometimes. I really go so that I can see Butterscotch. I can't believe no one has adopted him yet.

"Hey Prue, I hope you're having the best day so far."

"Hey you, I am. I've just been taking notes on what we'll be studying in each course."

"Cool, I was wondering. Do you mind coming to my place today instead? I have a few things that I'm finishing up here, and I want to cook some lunch."

"Okay, sounds good. Drop me your location."

"Alright, bet."

Well, that's different. Jemison's only been by my place a few times. We're usually out and about at different restaurants. I just realized I've never been to his apartment, not even once. I'm kind of curious to see how he lives. You can tell a lot about a person by their place no matter where they stay.

I wonder if he's the type to shove everything in his closet when people come over or if he hires a maid or has his mom come by to do his laundry. I hope he doesn't anticipate doing his laundry. I'm no fool. I am not providing wife duties to someone that's not my husband. Dating or not, single is single in the sense of "playing house." I guess I better pack up my laptop and notes and head over to JJ's.

It took me about half an hour to get over to JJ's place. I checked, and his apartment number was on the call box. I would have never imagined his apartment being this nice. Like, I like to think that my apartment is pretty nice, but Jemison's apartment looks like celebrities live upstairs in the penthouse.

There's a valet out here and everything. What the heck. I bet this place costs an arm and a leg. I know JJ works at a firm and all, but I didn't know that he was getting paid like this. Why is he working that part-time job then?

I walked in and was awestruck by the lobby. It had marble tiled floors where you literally see your reflection. And check out all these elevators. My building only has one, and it's mainly used by people with disabilities who don't already live on the first floor.

"Hey, you!" JJ said as he opened the door and welcomed me in.

"Oh wow, JJ, your place is beautiful," I whispered.

"Beautiful, come on, Prue. That would be your place."

"You know what I mean. It's so nice."

He laughed. "What, you expected me to live like some bum?"

"No, of course not," I giggled nervously. "I just didn't know what to expect."

"Yeah, I'm just giving you a hard time. Most people think guys are dirtbags. I get it. I personally can't live in chaos."

"I see. Shall we get started?" I asked.

"Sure, but let's have lunch first."

JJ's place is all that and some. Everything is so nice and neat. You would have thought this was a showroom or something out of a magazine. He has all black everything. It's what you would call decadent. I heard my mom say that word once when we were looking for furniture for my place.

JJ has beautiful marble and gold tables that sit nicely in front of his couch, facing a huge picture window. Nothing like my window that leads to the fire escape or the door leading to the patio. I also love the way his stairs are trimmed in gold, leading up to what looks like his bedroom.

"JJ, I absolutely love your place," I said as we sat down at his table. "You've done nicely for yourself."

"Thanks, but I can't take all the credit. My parents helped me pick out a few things. How do you like your lunch?"

I took another bite. "It's delicious! I didn't know you knew how to make sushi."

"Yeah, my aunt, my mom's sister, taught me. I thought it

would be nice to have tea while we look over the courses."

"Great idea. I see what you did there. I like it."

Cool, I was hoping so," he said.

"Here, I'll at least pull out my notes while we eat."

"So, there are a total of eight courses in the program. I started to explain. "I was shocked to see that. I know they're probably going to be hot and heavy, though. No pun intended." We both laughed. "Anyway, I'm looking forward to the course about sensory development and food pairing. I am so intrigued to learn how to bring out the tea's taste and its paired food. I'm sure we're going to be studying a lot, good thing there's nothing that really fills up my schedule. We got this. We can quiz each other. I bought some colored notecards, pens, and sharpies. I thought they would come in handy while we're studying."

JJ grinned. "Look at you, thanks, love."

The butterflies invaded my stomach again. "Anyway, like I was saying earlier, most of our courses are online. There are some opportunities for in-person consultancy courses. They're held in England and Kenya, though. Who has that kind of money? I'm not sure what the extra cost would be, but I'm already about to spend a pretty penny just on the certification courses alone. It would be a cool experience, though. Seeing other cultures and understanding how they live."

One thing I like about the tea sommelier website is that everything is spelled out for you. I haven't viewed the videos on the website yet, but I like the course schedule and the facts and answers to general questions. After we both looked at the website, we decided to study with the Tea & Herbal Association of Canada.

"I think we had enough for one day. Let's get you home beautiful," JJ said after a few hours of work.

I yawned and stretched. "Yeah, you're probably right. There's not much else to do until we decide on when to enroll for Tea 101. Let me get my things together."

As we walked hand in hand down the sidewalk, I didn't notice all the fire trucks screaming down the street. The smell of the smoke hit me two blocks before I saw the flames. I dropped JJ's hand and sprinted down the sidewalk, heart racing with the ground disappearing from under my feet. My building was engulfed in flames, smoke choking the air. Tears flowed from my face.

People are crowding the street, watching as the fire department tries to calm the fire waves. Everything that I have is in that apartment. My tea sommelier savings, gone. I hadn't had time to take my shoebox filled with tips to the bank yet.

This feels like a bad dream that I can't seem to shake myself awake from. What am I going to do? JJ has finally caught up to me. He's holding me tight from behind. He's saying something to me, and I must be in shock because I can't make out anything he's saying to me.

"There's nothing left," I finally whimper out loud. "OH MY GOD, JASMINE!"

Aroma

It's late. Stoke let me stay with her to be closer to work. I guess we're roommates now. It must have been fate that she never replaced her old roommate from last month. My mom's coming in the morning to bring me clothes and a few things for my new room. At least now living with Stoke, I don't have to buy new furniture. This is my way of coping… trying to find the silver lining.

The room is black. The only light shining in is a lamp from the living room that's barely shining under the door. Stoke's place is decent. It's set up a lot like mine was, the layout anyway. Our styles are very different. I'm sure I'll get used to it. I'm just grateful to be alive.

What if I were there in the apartment when it caught fire… what if JJ had been there with me? I'm trying to relax, but it's so hard. My mind is racing; I can't seem to get the cinder smells out of my nose. All I want to do is go to sleep, but I can't. I'm so used to Jasmine sleeping right next to me. I can't believe she's gone. I wish I would have allowed her to go outside while I was away. Maybe she would still be here. My pillow is soaked with tears…

Unable to sleep, I sat up writing the list of things I was grateful for. Let's see…I'm thankful for my life, my co-worker Stoke who's become a great friend, and the fact that I still have my laptop and don't have to buy a new one. I think those are all pretty great things. Oh, and for leaving lots of clothes at my mom's house. That way, I don't have many things to go out and buy.

I sat up writing so long that the sun came up. My stomach growled to remind me that I'm starving. I was in such a different state of mind last night that I didn't want to eat anything for dinner. I opened the door and stepped into the kitchen.

"Hey, Stoke."

"Good morning, my guh. I just put on some coffee. I thought you could use something a little stronger than tea this morning."

"You are right about that," I said as I sat down.

"Would you like some breakfast? I don't really cook breakfast foods, but we have leftover pizza."

"Girl, that is fine with me. I'm starving."

She smiled. "Well, go ahead, help yourself. This is your place too now. You might as well go ahead and start getting used to it."

"Yeah, you're right."

"Look, don't go getting all emotional on me. But come here, girl, hug me. It's going to be alright. You never know what blessings lie on the other side of tragedy."

She enveloped me in a huge hug. "I guess you're right. I'm just glad to be here."

"I know that's right. I'm glad you're here. I missed having a roommate."

I grabbed some leftover pizza from the fridge. "I'm glad to be here. It's going to be nice to have someone to walk to work with, at least on days we have the same shift."

"I know, right, me too, boo. Well, I'm going to leave you to it. I'm going to go shower and get ready," she disappeared out of the kitchen and into her bathroom.

Stoke is so great. I'm so thankful our lives crossed paths when they did. Life's funny. You never know what twists and turns lie before you.

Tears streamed down my face as I ate my pizza. I miss Jasmine so much. I've had her since my eleventh birthday. She was more than just a cat. She was my family. I hate she had to suffer like that and alone. But I can't dwell on her. I have to push myself through and get ready for work.

Living with Stoke will be fun. I'm glad each bedroom has it's own bathroom. It's nice to feel like I have my own space. I'm grateful to have a roommate, but it's nice to be totally secluded when I want to be. Besides coping with this fire, I'm sure I'll be in my room trying to figure out my new norm. I'm glad to be going to work today. It gives me a sense of normalcy. I want to feel like myself again.

Losing Jasmine and my apartment makes me feel like I just lost the person I was and was becoming all at once. I know that I am enough, but I have to figure out this new me. It's like I know who I am, but my routines have changed.

Walking into work, you would have thought that somebody died. My regulars must have heard about the fire because they all stood up to hug me once I put my apron on. Mrs. Judy and Mr. Tom both slipped me an envelope of money when they thought no one was looking. I hate feeling like some charity case, but I am very appreciative.

Just when I thought the day couldn't get any worse, Roman came down the stairs and threw his hands up in the air, grinning from ear to ear.

"Oh, Prue, darling. I am so glad that you're okay. If there is anything I can do, anything at all, just let me know," Roman said as he hugged me like I was his long-lost daughter.

"Thanks, Roman, but I'm fine, really."

"Well, know that I'm here for you if you need me for anything at all," he squeezed me tightly.

"Got it, thanks, Roman."

I'm glad to know that there are still good people in the world when tragedy strikes. I like how it always causes a community to band together, even if it is for a little while.

A few days later and work starts to feel normal now that everyone has stopped being so extra. I appreciate it, though. They could have gone on as business as usual, and I would have felt like no one cared. I'm sure I'll find a way to keep myself afloat. I would hate for my emotions to fall too deep where I can't get out.

Since all my money for my sommelier certification is gone, I don't even know if this is something that I can continue to pursue right now. So much for planning…never in a million years would I have imagined losing my apartment like that. I hadn't even been in it a whole year yet.

I'm glad JJ was with me. I probably would have been sitting in the middle of the street crying like a crazed maniac had he not been. He's a trooper. I know I had to have been a bit hysterical.

Kenny's voice shook me out of my reverie. "Hey Prue, I think your phone is going off in the back."

"Thanks, I must have forgotten to cut my ringer off. Let me grab it."

Aroma

"Hey chickadee, it's Momma."

"Mom, I know it's you," I rolled my eyes.

"Well, anyway, dear, are you feeling better?"

"Yeah, I'm good. It's just taking some getting used to."

"I know it is, sweetheart. I'm just glad you're okay. I was thinking, when you get off, how about you come to Brooklyn for dinner with me?"

"Okay, mom, I can do that."

"Great! Bring Stoke with you. That way, you do not have to go back alone."

"Couldn't I just bring JJ?"

"No, let's have a girls' night. In case you start crying, you can have a snot fest without being embarrassed in front of your new bae."

I chuckled. "Okay, Mom. You're right, even though I'm sure he had his share of my snot fest. It would be good to let my emotions fly without me being afraid to really let them loose."

"That's my girl."

"See you, girls, tonight. Steak."

"Shake."

"Bye, babe."

"Bye, Mom."

Got to love her. I'm starting to feel a little better already. There's nothing like a giant slice of pizza from Brooklyn's finest. I don't care what nobody says. New York pizza doesn't all taste the same.

Foreign

So, it turns out my mom took out Renters' Insurance on my apartment. Last month, when we met for dinner, she pulled out this envelope that looked like it had been in the mailbox for years. When I opened it, I was surprised to see that all my lost items were covered. Now that I live with Stoke, I don't have to replace anything major. This means I'll be using the extra money to fund my tea sommelier certification, and I can even participate in the in-person training overseas. I know! I can't believe it either!

After checking out all the overseas options, I've decided to go to England; it was the earliest and closest one available. Kenya doesn't' host another in-person course until next fall. I'm ready to complete this goal sooner than later. It is a part of my goal planning, you know. I feel like I have to do this for myself. I have to prove that I can lay out a plan and stick with it. I may be nervous, but I know I can do this, especially with all that I've just gone through.

The last few months have been something. At least it hasn't

been all bad. I have new friends who I love. A boyfriend and a job that keeps on giving.

Kenny and Stoke are taking me to the airport today. Kenny insisted on driving once he found out that JJ couldn't take me since he to work at an event. Jemison is trippin' because Kenny is taking me to the airport. The nerve of him, what would I look like dragging luggage around the city to catch a flight, a fool, homeless, I think not. Of course, I'm excited. This is an opportunity of a lifetime.

I do feel bad that Jemison can't go. He is the one that introduced me, after all. It feels wrong to be going without him. Stoke says I shouldn't guilt myself like that. It does make me wonder, though…if the shoe were on the other foot, would Jemison wait for me to be able to go with him or take the first flight out? Either way, I'm not going to linger on the what-ifs. I'm tired of always thinking of everyone else's feelings. This time, I want to do something for myself. I deserve to be selfish, even if it's just this once.

I had no idea what to pack for the trip. Thank God for Social Media so I could see what was trending. I'm definitely taking a pea coat. That was a no brainer. It's the beginning of November; it's not completely freezing, but it's chilly out for sure, and I refuse to get sick. Ain't nobody got time for that.

The buzzer rang, and I flew down the stairs. Kenny was waiting for me in his car.

"Thank you for agreeing to take me to the airport at the last minute. I really appreciate it," I said as I fastened my seatbelt.

"Don't mention it. You know I got you," Kenny replied with a goofy smirk.

"So, what are you looking forward to the most?" Stoke asked from the passenger seat.

"You know, I'm really not sure," I shrugged, clutching my bag. "I honestly don't have any expectations. I've never flown before, so I'm pretty excited about that."

"That's cool," Kenny glanced at me through the rearview. "I've never flown before either, so I'll be looking forward to hearing all about it once you get back."

Kenny pulled up in front of the passenger drop-off zone. I swallowed hard, and my palms are sweaty. Well, here goes nothing.

"Thanks for the ride, Kenny."

"Of course, you know I got you."

"You always do."

"Steak."

"Shake."

"Bye, bae."

"Alright, sweetie, you got this. Have fun. I'll see you," said Stoke as she hugged me good-bye.

Kenny's right. I should have fun. I shouldn't look at this trip as a strictly business. This must be memorable. It's not every day that I get to travel to another country on a plane.

Talk about culture shock. Boarding the plane is a whole ordeal. People are everywhere, and I'm trying to remember if I packed all of my toiletries. I don't know how many times I've stayed overnight somewhere and had to go out and buy a toothbrush.

A brunette lady is sitting in the middle seat in my row. I'm glad to have a window seat. I definitely would hate to be wedged between two strangers for the whole flight. When I took my seat, I immediately raised the shade to look out of the window. I would have never imagined the sky is so beautiful. Everything seemed so small when you're way up high. It's sad, really, that most of us spend our lives trapped in our own environments without exploring the world around us. I pulled out some gum to chew on so that my ears don't pop during take-off.

"Hi, I'm Prue, and you are?" I asked the lady next to me.

"Hello, my name is Cadence."

"Would you like some gum?" I offered her.

"Oh sure," she said, taking a piece. She was shaking slightly and noticed me staring. She shrugged. "Flights make me really nervous, and I forgot my lavender roll on."

I'm glad to know that I'm not the only one that is a little nervous about flying. Before we took off, she popped out her contacts like it's bad gum or something. She has a serious case of nerves. I sure hope she dozes off soon. She's really starting to weird me out.

As for me, the flight isn't so bad. The flight attendants served biscuits and tea once we were about halfway to our destination. I bet it's fun to be a flight attendant. They get to travel the world and even get paid for it. It must be nice. I imagine it's like living in a dream that you never wake up from.

After what seemed like forever on a plane ride, we finally landed. When I got off the plane, I can't believe my eyes. It's so beautiful here. Have you ever gone on a vacation for the summer or visit family out of town, and it felt like a dream? I used to get that feeling all the time as a little girl. It's like a dream in England, but I know that I am very much awake.

I spotted one of those people holding a sign that said, "The Cambridge School of Tea. I right walked up to him, and he asked my name. When I told him, he told me to wait for the others. Once we got all ten of us, Nigel escorted us to our bus and took us to The Cambridge School. Once there, we were given our room assignments. Lucky for me, I registered late and ended up with my own room. The campus is gorgeous! It looks like a museum. I enjoyed watching people along the river as I walked to my room. I felt at home. It was more than I could ever imagine. Once I got to my room, I put down my bags and headed to the common area to join the last-minute study group.

I'm glad there are some other Americans are on this trip. Although my classmates and I don't know each other well, it's nice to have some familiar faces around. Our schedules are jammed pack. We really won't get to sightsee much at all. At least I have an itinerary, so I'll know what to expect during training.

The last day and it's our all-day test day. It's only been an hour, and already the butterflies in my stomach are doing the cha-cha. What have I gotten myself into? I feel like just a baby tea nerd compared to everyone else. It's like everything that I had studied so far has just gone right out of the window. The instructor is very intimidating. She's like a meaner version of Meryl Streep from the movie *The Devil Wears Prada.* I kid you not. I'm trying to keep my face relaxed and not be an ugly American. But this lady is very, very intimidating. Like, her personality is like a rottweiler. It looks like she doesn't take crap from anybody.

I've completed most of my courses. We are covering the last class today and preparing for the final exam by going to a restaurant to practice cupping and naming the different tea types.

"Everyone takes a ticket from the basket," said the tea master from the center of the stage. I stood and tried to catch my breath. My stomach was beginning to quiver. This lady is talking, but I can't make out a thing that she's saying.

We are being called up by the numbers we pulled on our tickets. I'm just glad I'm not first so that I can see what we'll be doing, so I'm sure to do it the right way. I'm so nervous. I've never been one to get up and speak in front of the class without some hesitation and fear.

Some of these white tea names are throwing me for a loop. What did number two say, Darjeeling White? What is that? There was nothing in my guidebook about this. Let me check again. Well, here it is in plain black and white. How did I miss this one? I thought I've written out all the teas on my notecards. I feel like I'm about to have a panic attack.

"Pardon me," I said in a proper tone to the tea master. "May I use your powder room?" She glances in my direction, gesturing with her hand for me to go.

I nearly ran to the bathroom and splashed some cold water on my face. Okay, girl. Breathe, stretch, shake. Let it go. That's it. Breathe, stretch, shake; let it go. God, I ask that you bring all things back to my remembrance right now. In the name of Jesus, Amen.

I get back to the auditorium as the tea master called out my number. Well, here goes nothing.

"Take your pick and begin when you are ready," the tea master said as she looked down at her clipboard, ready to score.

I guess I'll take this one in the middle. No one has pulled the middle cup yet. I inhale the scent of the tea. As I exhale, I let out the biggest sigh of relief. All at once, my anxiety was gone, and a calmness captivated my whole body.

"Well then, are you ready?" asked the tea master.

"Yes, I am ready," I answered. "This is a Chinese green tea. It is high in polyphenols called catechins. This is a tea from the

Camellia sinensis plant. This is Jasmine, Chinese green."

"Very well," the tea master nods. What are the odds, right? My little princess is somewhere on the other side of that Rainbow Bridge looking out for me. I feel like she's helping me and wants me to do well.

Man, it's like I blinked, and it was over. Going to England was the best week of my life. The experience was everything. I may forget bits and pieces. Cups I identified. Questions that were asked. But I'll never forget how it made me feel. It felt familiar, like this is something that I was always supposed to do. I will miss it. I wish I were able to stay longer.

Roman sounded anxious for me to get back to work to share all the things I've learned over there. You should have heard him on the phone. Stoke and Kenny texted and Facetimed me every chance they got; they acted like I was never returning. It was only a week. I'm glad they were concerned, though. I love having friends like them. They're not just consumed by us having a good time together, but they are invested in what I'm doing and what I am passionate about.

Meh

I'm excited to get to work. Stoke and I stayed up all night when I finally got home talking about my trip. I've been home for a few days now, and I haven't seen Jemison much. He said that he's been busy working major events to pay for the rest of his courses. I know he's busy, but I miss him.

I don't get it. He barely even texted me while I was away. Grant it, I was always in a session when he texted. Plus, the time zone difference. I felt closer to him while overseas than I do being back home. I literally just left a foreign country where I never felt so at home. Coming back, Jemison never felt more unfamiliar.

"Um, hello, earth to Jemison." I snapped my fingers in front of his face.

"Yeah, sorry. What were you saying?"

"I was telling you about the cupping session."

He gave me a glazed smile. "Oh, right. Right, go ahead."

The conversation with Jemison was so dry. I couldn't wait to leave his place.

I don't know what his deal is lately. Every time I talk to him, he seems so uninterested in the words coming out of my mouth. I feel like something is going on with him. We used to talk about everything and laugh for hours and hours. Now it's like he's pulling away from me.

Whatever. I don't have time for all this guessing with him right now. I'm so focused on the teahouse and utilizing my new certification.

I passed my final exam! No negative vibes here. Call it what you want. By offering the world good energy, I'm sure nothing but positive vibes are to follow.

Jemison and I have finally compromised some things in our schedule so that we could have time to go on a few dates. It's been pretty cool. I can't really fault him for not spending as much time together as we used to. We've both been pretty busy with work and all. I try not to be so clingy, but I really enjoy JJ's company.

I've been trying to be more low-key in our relationship. Instead of insisting on us chilling and going out, I've been allowing him to take the lead on things. It's been saving your girl's feelings.

Now, I wait for him to make that call whenever he finds time in his schedule. Talk about a change of pace. Since putting the ball in his court, we haven't seen each other nearly as much as I would like to.

Besides, when we do hang out, we're either with his friends or colleagues from work. They are all so different from the usual scene. I've started inviting Kenny and Stoke out with us to have—well, fun. That way, I'm sure to have a good time and be around people I actually like. I feel like I've been trying to fit into this mold that Jemison set for me.

Meh

Before this relationship, I used to tell myself if I must fake a smile, I'm not going. It takes up so much energy when you're having to fake. Jemison's people aren't the friendliest. They're very judgmental, and hearing them talk trash about people, especially innocent bystanders, is getting old really quick.

On top of that, Jemison's treated me more like the homie than his girlfriend. Call me crazy, but this dude seems like he's putting me in the friend zone—crazy, right? I could just be blowing things way out of proportion. I can see that he wants me to get to know his world just like I want him to know mine.

I probably need to start going to yoga with Roman more than once a week. It will do me some good for sure. I feel like I've been so tense lately when it comes to Jemison.

I mean, really. Jemison must be under a great deal of pressure with trying to complete his tea sommelier certification on top of working two jobs, all while trying to juggle a relationship with me. Now that I've said that out loud, that's probably exactly what it is. Jemison is probably stretching himself thin to please everybody. Maybe that's why his friends are always around now for most of our dates. Jemison probably hasn't had time to spend with either of them as well.

OMG! I'm totally selfish. Here I want Jemison all to myself to hear me rant and rave about what I'm doing that I didn't even consider the fact he must be so tired and want to relinquish to the silence of us just being present with each other. Hmm. I wonder what I could do for him to make him happy. I know! I can make him a man bouquet with all of his favorite things. I'm sure that will make his day. I could also take him to that new tea spot he likes—my treat.

I better get to work. I'm just ecstatic to see all the guests today. Plus, I want to try out my new skills, including offering everyone various pastries to match their tea of choice.

There are so many teas and treat combinations that I have come up with. Roman has decided to create a small brochure to list them all in once it's just right. That way, we won't lose any customers by taking too long to help them decide which pastry to have with their tea. They'll be able to choose themselves and be ready to place their order. The possibilities are endless. I love seeing their faces even more now when they enjoy a warm tasty treat to wash down with a nice hot tea.

Kenny and Stoke have been getting along better since I've been back. I'm glad that they're not killing the teahouse vibe with all their negative energy. I'm used to them arguing and roasting each other with me left there to make them hash it out. Let's be clear, though. It's so much more fun now that we're all joking and laughing together all the time.

I wonder what made them reconcile their differences. I won't be asking them, though. I'm curious, but I'm not nosey. It's none of my business anyway.

I better go ahead and get started on my closing checklist. Kenny agreed to buy a few small bourbon bottles for Jemison's man bouquet since he's twenty-one. Kenny's not much of a drinker even though he's old enough to. He says he just never had the urge to go out and drink all the time just because he can. He may have one or two drinks max on a given occasion, but that's it. I admire him so much for that.

Milk

"Cheers!" I tell Jemison as we clank our boba teas together. "The perfect date with the perfect man. Gosh, I missed you so much," I said as I rested my hand on top of his.

"Me too, love," he replied. "Prue, you should have really tried this Strawberry Avocado with me. It's pretty good."

"I like the unicorn one. It's just the right amount of sweetness and grape flavoring."

"Suit yourself. You don't know what your missing," he said as he swirled his cup in my face.

"Today's going to be great," I assured him.". I thought that we go over to the animal shelter and play with Butterscotch, go axing, and then a little Netflix minus the chill back at my place. Don't worry. Stoke will be out tonight, so it'll be just the two of us."

"Well, yes, ma'am," he said as he saluted me.

I don't know whether to laugh or feel insulted by that or not. I hope he doesn't think I'm too forward in planning this day for him. I thought he would like the fact of me taking the initiative to do something kind for him. I hope he sees my heart and knows that my intentions are good.

I wouldn't say I like that the newness of Manhattan has finally worn off. I guess that's the feeling of being officially sworn in as a local. After we finish our Boba tea, we head to the animal shelter.

"After you," Jemison says as he opens the door. Walking through the building, the barks almost drowned out my thoughts. I bet they're happy to have someone here to play with them. These dogs have really grown on me.

"Where's Butterscotch?" I asked the shelter worker.

"Oh, he's been adopted. He's been gone for a few weeks now, sorry, Hun," she said.

"Wow, a few weeks ago, Jemison, why didn't you tell me?"

"What, it was nothing to tell," Jemison shrugged. "It's an animal shelter. It's not like he was going to be here forever." He kneeled to hook a leash to another dog to walk outback.

I'm just at a loss for words. I really liked that dog. Jemison was so nonchalant about it. But I guess he has a point. It's not like Butterscotch belonged to either one of us. I guess I had become emotionally attached to him. I guess spending time with the dogs here is feeling the void of losing Jasmine. I miss her. It doesn't hurt me to think of her nearly as bad as it uses to.

After my date with Jemison, I couldn't wait for Stoke to come home so that I could spill my own tea.

"Asking Jemison why he didn't tell me about Butterscotch was a stupid thing to say, right?" I asked her.

"Girl, please, you have a right to feel however you want to feel about whatever. What's gotten into you?" she asked.

"I don't know," I shrugged. "I guess I feel like I can't do or say anything right around Jemison anymore. It's like he sees me as this naïve girl."

"Hmm, that's crazy. Whatever it is, it's not you, so stop it," she said as she got up to brew us a cup of tea. "Listen, Prue, I'm not a love expert or anything, but I know when something isn't right. What I'm saying is keep going over there with him drinking your little boba tea and feeling like you're talking to a brick wall. Just like my granny used to say, something in the milk ain't clean."

"Stoke, now what does that even mean?"

"It means that something is definitely not right," she explained.

I'm starting to think Stoke's right. I have done nothing but gone out of my way for Jemison. Now that I think about it, my heart doesn't even feel like it's beating right out of my chest when he looks at me. He stares at me coldly instead of with infatuation. Maybe I should tell him how I feel. It's not like he's a mind reader. Plus, guys can be idiots. He probably doesn't even know he's been coming off a certain way.

Why do I keep making excuses for him? I'm tired of going in circles with him. Especially when I feel like I'm going through all of this alone. I wonder if he's gotten bored with me.

You know what. I'm not doing this anymore. I'm not going to obsess over something that I can't control. I'm honestly tired to death of it. This situation is really messing with my vibe.

Feeling unwanted is really bogging me down. You know what, enough—is enough. I'm too exhausted to call him tonight. I think I'll go over and see him first thing before work tomorrow.

"I'm officially sleepy now," I said to Stoke as I unwrapped from my blanket. "I'm out, girl. Steak."

"Shake," she says back.

"Goodnight, boo," I tell her as I head off to my room.

Wither

With all that happened yesterday, I had a pretty good night's rest. You ever had absolute peace about something, knowing that somehow, it's all going to work out just fine? Well, that's exactly how I feel. It's just an unexplainable joy.

I feel so good. I may even go for a jog this morning. Why not—I deserve a change of scenery. Especially in this nice weather.

I checked my cell and noticed that JJ texted me.

"Prue, I'll be in the office today. I have a few deadlines to meet, so I'll get up with you later—cool."

What, get up with me later? He never talks like that. That's so random. I'm not letting him get to me—not today.

I'm just going to lace up these shoes, put on this waist trainer, and get my run on.

"Hey, Stoke!" I called out.

"Yeah, girl, what's up?"

"I'm heading out for a run. I'll be back in a bit."

"Alright, girl. Steak."

"Shake."

"Bye, bae!" We both yell as I'm heading out the door.

I'm just going to take it nice and slow. You know, just a little light jog. I've never been much of a runner. Conner and Mila were more of the track stars. I only joined the team so that we would all be together. Silly, I know. But I didn't want to be left out whenever they had practice or track meets.

Whew, here we go. This isn't bad at all. Maybe I'll pick up the momentum a little bit. I'm definitely not going to sprint along the sidewalk. If I did, I'm sure I'll knock somebody down. Just my luck, it could be some older man or lady, then I'll be looking at a lawsuit.

I can see it in the headlines now. Thick Girl Tramples the Elderly Near Central Park. I know. Kind of farfetched, but you smell what I'm cooking. I think I've worked up a thirst. I might as well stop and grab a Boba tea since it's in the area.

I walked in and was greeted by the barista behind the counter.

"Hey, Prue! How are you?"

"Now, this is just sad. You know you go somewhere too often when the workers start calling you by name."

"I'm well. How are you, Brian?"

"Doing pretty good."

"That's great. I would like the usual."

"Of course. You do love the Unicorn." Brian started making my drink, talking to me the whole time. "Fancy seeing you here."

"Really, why is that?"

Brian paused for just a second before he handed me my drink. "We saw Jemison here just a little while ago. You two usually come in together."

"Yeah, he's pretty busy with work today."

"Oh, okay."

Call me crazy, but I could have sworn Brian just made a side-eye. We can't always be together. It's not like we're joined by the hip. I'm not even sure we're connected by the heart at this point.

"Thanks for the tea," I tell Brian as I raise my cup as I walk out of the door. I refuse to allow anything to disrupt this beautiful day. You know what, though. I must be honest. I am a little bothered by Brian's side-eye gesture. Like, really. What was that all about. It seems like he knows something I don't.

That's it. I'm done. That's all I have to say about that. I'm not even about to tell that lie like I'm not going to ask Jemison about it. I'm not a crazed psycho girlfriend by no means. If the situation presents itself, I'll ask. But until then, I refuse to allow it to consume my day.

Woosah.

Deep breaths. Good thing I brought my lavender roll on. No stomach quivering today. Aht, aht. No ma'am, no ham, no turkey, no burger. I'm not doing this. I'll go on home. Have a little facial. Pop me some kettle corn and watch a movie. Nothing like a little self-care Saturday.

Besides, Stoke is at the tea house today, so I'll have a little me time until she gets home tonight. I haven't quite figured out what to say to Jemison after yesterday. But what I do know is this conversation must be had sooner rather than later.

Maybe I should run back to clear my head. My goodness, why am I running like someone is chasing me? Good thing I remembered to put on Vaseline this morning. Cause Lord knows these thighs would be burning out of control otherwise. Go ahead and laugh. You know it is real out here for us thick girls. I'm not even ashamed, though. I always sing in my head, "Slim, thick with Yo cute ahh…WHAT THE HELL!?!?

I HAVE TO BE DREAMING!!! THIS IS A NIGHTMARE!!! You know what FORGET THIS AND FORGET HIM!!!! AND FORGET RUNNING AT THIS POINT I'M WALKING HOME. I'm out of breath anyway…

Refresh

I'm not sad…yet here I am. Crying on the floor of the shower. The water rushing along my head is drowning out, even my inner thoughts. For once, I'm not thinking. Just melting in my own pot of selfless rage. Calm rage. Which doesn't even make sense. Maybe it's not rage at all. I'm just—here. Not a word to be said. Not a thought to be had. I'm just—here. Soaking in the reality of what is.

For once, I am present with myself. Taking it all in. Feeling what's to be felt. Yet, my heart is beating at a steady pace. Not too fast, not too slow, just constant. Allowing me to live. Not exist as a passive senseless being, taking up space with no purpose.

I'm all cried out. I guess I'm deciding that I don't want to waste another tear. I don't want to cry another minute. Not for something or someone that is so obsolete. So there, there it is. I'm still sitting here in this shower as if I'm in the middle of an ocean with no lifesaver insight. I'm not even sure why I'm crying. I'm not even sad. Sure, I was in a rage, but who isn't when they are suddenly awakened to something that seems to be right in front of them all along.

I guess my mind is finally coming back to the present. The room is dark. The only light in this bathroom is from a candle. The dark can't help but relent. This shower was just what I needed. Not my face mask. Not Kettle corn. Not even a movie.

Well, it's time for me to pull myself together. No sense in crying over spilled milk, especially if it was never clean or whatever Stoke said. There is a knock on the bathroom door.

"Yeah?"

"Hey Prue, JJ's here."

"Okay, tell him I'll be out in a minute."

"Alright, girl."

As I turned off the shower and grabbed my towel, I have this silly smirk plastered on my face. I can't help but giggle now. There's no frog in my throat. No stomach quivering. I never thought about what I would say to Jemison. I guess things sometimes have a way of working themselves out. It's like all of a sudden. These words are just filling my head and waiting to spew out right into Jemison's lap. I got dressed and walked out into the living room where Jemison was waiting for me.

"Well, hello Jemison, what are you doing here?"

"I saw you today, and I wanted to come by to talk."

I raised my eyebrow and laughed. "To talk about what? To talk about how you were tonguing down some Kimora Simmons looking girl, and we have only given each other no more than a peck on the lips."

Jemison grabbed my wrist. "Prue, wait!"

"Wait? You know what, you're right. That's what I should have done when I first saw you in the tea house. Waited…When I first saw you, I thought I was cautious, using wisdom and good judgment. But instead, I was blinded by the steam from the tea that your hubristic ego was brewing."

"See, this is why we don't work," Jemison huffed at me.

"And why is that?"

He sighed. "Because you're a "teaholic" who can't see past the steam in your own eyes since you want to use tea analogies."

"Excuse me, what exactly is that supposed to mean, Jemison?"

"It means that ever since you got your little certification or whatever, everybody's been blowing hot air up your ass, and you think you're hot shit. You wouldn't even know what a sommelier was if it wasn't for me."

"Really? You're going to play that game?" I clapped back.

"That's just it, Prue. This isn't a game for me. For you, this may be a little gap year fun, but for me, this is my life. This is what I want to do. We were supposed to do this together. But you forgot that you forgot about us."

I held up my hand. "Let me stop you right there. Yes, if it weren't for you, I wouldn't have known what a sommelier was, and for that, I thank you, but hell. What do you want a cookie? I'm the one that stayed up countless hours studying, cupping, and learning. Not just memorizing information long enough to receive my 'little certificate.' It's not little to me. I earned it. I would think you would've been happy for me, but now I see this has been all about you. Is this what little miss thing was all about?"

"At least she sees me," Jemison snapped. "Ever since you started pursuing the sommelier certification, it's been all about you."

"What you're not going to do is play the guilt trip on me for becoming passionate about something that I learned to love."

"Girl, bye."

"Ha-ha, you're so funny. You never talk like this. It's like you've been putting on a front this whole time, and now your mask has finally fallen," I shook my head. "You know what, I don't owe you an apology, but I am sorry. I'm sorry that your parents have given you a world on a silver platter, and now that they've cut you off and things are becoming 'hard' for you, you don't seem to know what to do. I'm not going to sit around stroking your ego just because you didn't pass your certification. I did all I could to help you besides take the exam for you."

"You know what, Prue, forget you!"

I grinned widely. "You couldn't forget me even if you tried. I'm thankful for you, Jemison, and I wish you well. Now leave."

"Oh fa'sho, I'm out," Jemison turned and slammed the door behind him on the way out. When I turned around, Stoke was standing there with a goofy look on her face, and her arms opened wide.

"Oh my gosh, Stoke, what are you doing?"

"Steak," she said.

"Shake."

"BABY BYE!" We both yelled as we burst out into laughter.

"Are you okay?"

"Yeah. I am," I giggled. "I couldn't be better, actually."

"I knew he was faulty. I knew it."

"If you knew it, then why didn't you tell me?"

"Girl, you were so, gone," Stoke shrugged. "I figured you'd eventually figure it out on your own."

"Yeah. I guess you're right. The crazy thing is, I don't think we should have been dating in the first place."

"Yep, that's true too," Stoke put her arm around my shoulder. "But hey, he was just a traveler on your journey. You learned something new that you might have not otherwise, becoming a sommelier and knowing a counterfeit bachelor when you see one."

I chuckled. "I'm thankful. I'm not even sad, really. More relieved, if anything. No one needs a guy like that. He's so arrogant and consumed with himself. I honestly wish him well. He's obviously miserable."

Stoke rolled her eyes. "That's sweet of you, Prue, always finding that silver lining."

There was a knock on the door, and we both jumped a bit. I got up and looked through the peephole.

"What is Kenny doing here?" I whispered to Stoke.

"Why don't you open the door?" She whispered back.

I threw open the door. "Kenny, hey, what are you doing here?"

"Hey, I wanted to come and see you, and I brought a friend."

"Oh, my goodness!" I knelt and hugged the furry dog around the neck. "Butterscotch! Kenny, how did you?"

"May I come inside?"

I stood up, still holding on to Butterscotch. "Yes, yes, I'm sorry. Come on in."

"Hey Stoke, what's good?"

"I'm chillin," she smirked as Butterscotch sat on the rug and thumped his tail. I joined him on the floor to pet him and looked at Kenny, who sat next to Stoke. Stoke made an excuse to go to the kitchen.

"Kenny, so you adopted Butterscotch?"

"Yes, listening to you talk about him all the time really made me want to give him a home. A forever home."

I scratched the dog's ear. "I didn't even know you were paying attention to me like that."

Kenny flushed. "Truth is Prue. I've always paid attention to you. Everything about you. Like how you love peppermint tea, but you started drinking more Jasmine tea after losing Jasmine, or how your eyes slightly close when you smile. I even noticed how you always run off to the bathroom every time you're nervous. I've also noticed how you also see the good in others. So much so that sometimes you're not aware when a wolf appears in sheep's clothing."

I stared at him. "Kenny, what are you doing? You're like a brother to me."

He slid off the couch, and Butterscotch thumped his tail and laid his head on his lap. "But see, that's just it, I'm not. You put me in the friend zone as soon as you met me. Back then, you were focused. See, I knew that you needed room to grow. I never wanted to get in the way of that."

"What? I honestly don't know what to say."

"Say that you will go out to lunch with me after Yoga on Wednesday."

"Kenny, that's sweet, and I would love to actually, but don't you usually cover that shift with Stoke?"

"I did, but while you were away, Roman opened up a new nutrition tea and boba tea bar. Thanks to you. I'll be running the store for him as the head manager."

"WHAT!" I yelled. Stoke poked her head out from the kitchen and gave me a thumbs up. "That's amazing. Why didn't either one of you tell me?'

"To be honest, I wanted to wait. You see, Prue. Timing is everything. I knew you weren't ready to handle a man like me yet. Life is filled with chances and choices. You may have chosen him, but now I'm asking that you take a chance with me."

I stifled a giggle that escaped my mouth, and Kenny frowned. "Why are you laughing?"

I clapped my hand over my mouth. "Sorry, it's not funny. It's just a thing I do now in serious situations."

"So, what do you say?" Kenny stood up and held out his hand to help me up.

"I guess I'll see you Wednesday."

"Alright, bet. I'll bring Butterscotch. I know you two have some catching up to do."

"That's sweet."

"Well, I guess I'll see you then. Alright, Stoke," Kenny said as he walked out the door.

"What was that?" I asked Stoke as she came in with two cups of tea and sat down on the couch next to me. "Talk about timing."

"Well, I kind of helped with that."

I felt the heat go up to my neck. "Stoke, did you tell him to come over here?"

She nodded before covering her face with the pillow.

I pulled the pillow away. "Why would you do that? You know Kenny is like a brother to me."

"But as he said, Prue, he's not," she sighed. "The truth is Kenny has liked you for a while now. Not initially, though. You kind of grew on him. He's always liked you as a person but not like you know, like you, like you. Remember the day you came back to the tea house, and the tension was so thick you could cut it with a knife?"

"Yeah."

"Well, Kenny and I were arguing like we always do, and I took it too far. I told Kenny he was on his man cycle and mad because he would rather be out with you, but instead, you were out with JJ. That's when I found out that he really had a thing for you. I must have really hurt his feelings, too, because he wouldn't even look at me. He didn't even have so much of a snarky comment."

"Stoke, why didn't you tell me?" I groaned.

"You never want us to spill the tea."

"Come on, Stoke, it's different when the tea is about me. I need some air. I'll be on the balcony."

I stepped out on the balcony and started laughing. I guess it's true. The pain of today does open up doors of joy for tomorrow. Today has taken me for a loop.

Me and Kenny, Kenny, and me. I can't even grasp it all yet. One thing is for sure, though. I'm down with it. Why not? Kenny and I have known each other for almost a year. He already knows how I eat and how I act. I won't have to walk on eggshells with him or pretend to be something I'm not. Besides, anyone that is that invested and knowing me like that deserves a shot.

I'm flattered, really, especially with all this crap with Jemison. Maybe he and "Miss Simmons" will work out. But if she knows as I know, she will shoot for the nearest train and ride back to wherever she's from. Maybe it was a good thing that Mom never got a chance to meet him in person. I think that would complicate things.

Once someone you're dating meets your people, the relationship turns into a whole investment, like on an entirely different level. Your home is your sanctuary. You shouldn't allow everyone in. Once you meet family, you too become part of my family.

Ending things with Jemison is like stretching out your limbs after yoga, refreshing. Jemison may have released me into orbit, but now I'm gravitating towards Kenny. Jemison and I merely grew apart. There's no sense in me not allowing myself to see where things go with Kenny.

At least I don't have to worry about being put in the friend zone. Kenny is already the homie. I think the two of us being friends first makes it that much easier. Some girls won't ever cross this line for fear of ruining a friendship. But what if, what if dating your friend adds to your friendship?

It's been a season of choice and chances, for sure. I'll decide whether this experience with dating Kenny is a good idea or not. You never know unless you try. No doubts. No fears. Just compliments without tears.

I'm learning how to make mistakes. Embracing the changes that better me as a person. Mistakes aren't a failure, but rather an avenue for learning. For so long, I've tried to do everything just right. Playing it safe, learning from other people's mistakes. Not once did I consider learning from the mistakes of my own.

I now believe that learning from your own mistakes is better. I think it's because you've gone through it. I walked it out, feeling every bit of the momentum to succeed as well as the faltering heart pains that come when you have missed the mark.

Either way, I'm grateful. For Jemison, the fire, Jasmine's loss, and the non-existing plan, I'm thankful, I'm grateful, I'm blessed. There are so many good things in my life. I can't help to accept them all. Taking the good with the bad, it's my life to be had. I might as well embrace it all.

Like Mom says, no matter how bad you may think things are, it could always be worse, and there are others out there that wish that they could be standing right in your shoes. It's sad to think about it like that, I know, but you must admit, it's true. There is no one else I'd rather be nor a place that I'd rather go. Well, except for Brooklyn for pizza night with good ole Pat. You know, I love my mom. On that note, I can go to bed—at peace. Finally.

Reliant

During the night, as I was blissfully sleeping, Connor left a text. She's coming home for winter break and was coming to visit me today. AHHH!! I'm so, so excited. I have missed her so much.

We have texted a few times, but we most definitely didn't talk as often as we would have liked to. I can't wait to hear all about her classes and the people she's met. I especially want to hear all about campus life. I know Connor had that dorm room decked out. I wonder if she talks any different since being in the south. Connor may have enjoyed it so much that she may not want to come back.

"STOKE!" I yelled from the room.

"YO!" she yelled back.

"TEA! PLEASE!"

Stoke is my girl. It's been so great living here with her. There's never a dull moment with the two of us together. She's become more than a co-worker and roommate. She's been a great friend. Better yet, a sister. I'm honestly glad to have her. She's definitely held it down through some callous times this year.

I always wondered what it would be like to have a sister. Now I do, tons of fun and endless laughter. We're pretty lucky, I guess. We never fight over anything. I know not to touch her Twizzlers, and she knows if she lays one finger on my Oreos, she might as well have her momma plan her funeral. Okay, I'm joking, of course. Oreos are good, but it most certainly is not anything to want to hurt, let alone kill someone over it.

I walked out of the bedroom and into the kitchen where Stoke was sitting with two cups of tea. I sat and took a sip of mine, closing my eyes, and inhaling the smell.

"Mmhhh, this tea is so good. Lavender vanilla has really become my thing. It's calming and relaxing." I glanced down at my phone and lit up. "Connor just texted me and said that she would be here soon. Oh, Stoke, I can't wait!"

I felt like a kid on Christmas day. I wonder if she looks any different. You know, college is where some people go and rediscovered themselves, then return home to reintroduce themselves to their families. At least that's what I see in movies. It's amusing, honestly. Where is that girl??

What is taking her so long? She said she was headed up like she was literally downstairs. I called her because I was so impatient.

"Hey girl, where are you?"

"Walking towards your door."

"Oh, yay! Okay, bye."

The door knocked, and I threw it open and grabbed Connor for a huge hug. "Hey, girl! Oh my gosh, it's been way, way too long get in here."

"Hold on, let me grab my bags."

"Your bags?"

She stepped in with some luggage. "Yeah, I wanted to ask you and Stoke in person."

"Ask us what?" Stoke and I asked.

"Can I stay with y'all?"

"For winter break, cool?" I looked at Stoke and shrugged. "Are you going to your parents on Christmas and New Year's?"

"No, I want to stay with y'all as in live here?"

"WHAT?" Stoke and I both yelled in surprise.

"I mean, I can stay on the couch. Just for a little while. I don't want to put anybody out," Connor said a little nervously.

"Well, of course, you can."

"Come on in," Stoke said as we sat on the couch and Connor sat on the chair. "We can talk about the details. How long do you plan to stay with us?"

Connor settled back in the armchair. "I guess until I get a job and save some money to at least pay for the deposit and first months rent for a place of my own."

"That's a good plan. It seems like you had some time to think this through." I frowned a little. "Wait, Connor, you care to tell us what's going on? Why aren't you at your parents' house? I thought you all would be glad to see each other during the holidays?"

Connor sighed and ran her hand up and down her arm. "Well, that's just it. I'm really not speaking with them right now. They've completely cut me off."

"What? Why?" Stoke asked.

"Yeah, what about college?" I echoed.

"Child, college was not my cup of tea."

About the Author

Alexandria Cunningham is a teacher, Alzheimer's advocate, and writer. She lives in Alabama with her husband, Kirstan, and spoiled dog, Kemper Kai. She is the founder of Inspiring Honey Publishing LLC with an imprint called Funky Fresh Nerds. Alexandria is the author of the children's book Honey's Dance Recital. Hot Tea and Laughter is her first novella.

Also by Alexandria Cunningham

Children's Honey Book Series

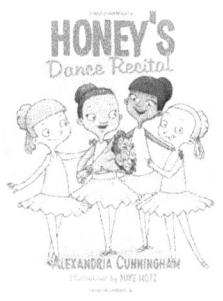

Honey's Dance Recital

Meet Honey, a sassy southern biracial dance fanatic who speaks in rhyme all the time. Honey loves to snack and enjoys southern cooking, almost as much as she enjoys the ballet. In this sweet and spicy tale, follow Honey, a six-year-old perfectionist, and her friends as they prepare for their big show.

CPSIA information can be obtained
at www.ICGtesting.com
Printed in the USA
LVHW112145060921
697168LV00017B/466

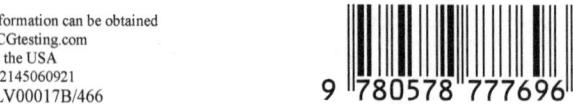